PUFFIN BOOKS

Into Exile

Joan Lingard was born in Edinburgh but grew up in Belfast where she lived until she was eighteen. She began writing when she was eleven, and has never wanted to be anything other than a writer. She is the author of more than twenty novels for young people and thirteen for adults. Joan Lingard has three grown-up daughters and three grandchildren, and lives in Edinburgh with her Latvian/Canadian husband.

Joan Lingard

Into Exile

PUFFIN

PUFFIN BOOKS

Published by the Penguin Group
Penguin Books Ltd, 80 Strand, London WC2R 0RL, England
Penguin Putnam Inc., 375 Hudson Street, New York, New York 10014, USA
Penguin Books Australia Ltd, 250 Camberwell Road, Camberwell,
Victoria 3124, Australia
Penguin Books Canada Ltd, 10 Alcorn Avenue, Toronto, Ontario, Canada M4V 3B2
Penguin Books India (P) Ltd, 11 Community Centre, Panchsheel Park,
New Delhi – 110 017, India
Penguin Books (NZ) Ltd, Cnr Rosedale and Airborne Roads, Albany, Auckland,
New Zealand
Penguin Books (South Africa) (Pty) Ltd, 24 Sturdee Avenue, Rosebank 2196,
South Africa

Penguin Books Ltd, Registered Offices: 80 Strand, London WC2R 0RL, England

www.penguin.com

First published by Hamish Hamilton 1973
Published in Puffin Books 1974
Reprinted in Penguin Books 1988
Reissued in Puffin Books 1995, 2003
12

Copyright © Joan Lingard, 1973
All rights reserved

Filmset in Monotype Bembo

Made and printed in England by Clays Ltd, St Ives plc

Except in the United States of America, this book is sold subject to the condition that
it shall not, by way of trade or otherwise, be lent, re-sold, hired out, or otherwise
circulated without the publisher's prior consent in any form of binding or cover other
than that in which it is published and without a similar condition including this
condition being imposed on the subsequent purchaser

British Library Cataloguing in Publication Data
A CIP catalogue record for this book is available from the British Library

ISBN 0–140–37213–X

Chapter One

Sadie McCoy stood by the window looking out into the dingy street. It was Sunday morning, early, and few people were about, which made the street look even worse than usual. She was used to dingy streets, it was not that in itself that was bothering her, but the streets she had known were Belfast ones, with straight rows of red-bricked houses built back to back. This was a London street, and even after a month it still looked foreign to her.

She pulled the yellowish-white net back to the edge of the window so that she could see a bit farther. A black man came round the corner carrying a newspaper. There was no sign of Kevin. She sighed, dropped the net back into place. He had gone to mass. She did not like him going; she felt uneasy all the time he was away. She had dreams in which black-robed priests tried to hold on to Kevin and would not let him leave the church even when he wanted to. He laughed when she told him about the dreams and said she believed too many of the old wives' tales about Catholics that she'd been told as a child. She was a Protestant. That was why they had come to London.

She filled the kettle at the small sink in the corner of the room, lit the gas ring and set the water to boil. She did all her cooking on this one ring. The landlady had promised another, but that was when they had first come, and now when Sadie asked about it Mrs Kyrakis looked vague and her English failed her. She was a Greek Cypriot but had been in London a long time, and her English failed her only at opportune

5

moments. Fourteen people lived in her house, like rabbits in warrens, each tucked away in their separate holes, and downstairs in one room at the back Mrs Kyrakis slept and ate and collected her money. She was seen only on Friday evening, rent night.

It was a waste of time to bang on her door on any other day. And it was a waste of time to ask for anything. She would say, as she took the rent into her thick hands and began to count, 'I see about it', and then forget until the following Friday. They paid a lot of money to live in this one miserable room. At least it seemed a lot to Sadie and Kevin for they were used to Ulster prices. At home they could have had a whole house for the same money. In some parts of Belfast you could have a house for nothing. But that was because you could get a bullet through your head to go with it. So they paid their money and thankfully closed their door and no one bothered them. Here they had peace.

Sadie scooped a spoonful of tea into the pot and put it near the flame to warm, then took two cups down from the shelf. Kevin should be in at any moment and he would be dying for a cup of tea. He had gone out without breakfast. She had been lying beside him warm and snug in the old sagging bed which took up one wall of the room. 'Do you have to go?' she had asked him, knowing that he would go for he always did.

'I don't have to. But I feel better when I do.'

'Ach, don't go this morning, Kevin. Just this once!'

He had lain awhile and then got up. She had sat up and pouted at him.

'Are you feared of what your mammy might say? But she's not here to see you. Or is it the priest you're feared of?'

She had a terrible tongue on her, she knew it full well. There were times when it just seemed to run away with her. Kevin had been mad with her, and they had had a row. That was why she was so restless now, going to the window every

6

two minutes to see if he was coming. What if he didn't come back? She closed her eyes, panic seizing her at the idea. Her ma had always said that her tongue would get her into real trouble one day.

Sadie opened her eyes and looked round the room, at its shabby broken furniture, the peeling wallpaper, the damp patch near the window that looked like an elephant, the torn linoleum, and her new red rug. If he was to abandon her here alone! Alone in this street. In this city. This enormous sprawling noisy city where she knew no one but Kevin.

A passing figure blocked the light from the window momentarily. She heard Kevin's feet. As he came into the hallway of the house she flung open the door of the room.

'Kevin!' she cried, throwing her arms round his neck. 'I thought you weren't coming back.'

'Not coming back!' He made a funny face at her. 'And where did you think I'd gone? Buckingham Palace?'

She laughed. Of course he wouldn't have left her! They went into the room.

'I'm a real head case,' she said.

'You can say that again!'

'I'm sorry about this morning.'

'That's all right!' He grinned at her. 'I knew you would be after I'd gone.'

The kettle was boiling, clouding the room with steam. She poured the water into the tea pot.

'Would you like some ham and egg?' she asked.

'I certainly would. I'm starved.'

He lay back on the bed whilst she fried the bacon and eggs. The smell filled the room making their mouths water. The room would smell for the rest of the day but they did not bother about that now. When they went to bed at night Sadie would sniff the air and say, 'I hate sleeping with the smell of cooking round my face.'

'There!' she said, flipping Kevin's egg out on to the plate, and as she did so she thought of her mother standing in the kitchen at home in her flowered wrap-around overall doing the very same thing. Bacon and egg: her mother cooked more of that than anything else.

'What are you thinking about?' asked Kevin, looking up at her.

'Me ma,' said Sadie, mocking herself a little.

'Aye.' Kevin sighed. 'It'd be fine to see our families once in a while.'

Sadie was not sure that she wanted to see hers. She had written to her mother after she and Kevin had been married at Gretna Green in Scotland, and her mother had written back to tell Sadie that she had broken her heart. Sadie didn't believe that fully for her mother always exaggerated, especially when it came to the bad things in life. The good things she tended to underestimate. She would sniff cautiously at a good piece of news and say, 'Yes, well, but – ' Kevin had written to his family too and his sister Brede had written back to say that she hoped they would be very happy together. But Brede was young, only seventeen, the same age as Sadie, and also she knew Sadie and they liked one another. Kevin said he thought his mother would wish them well but would be afraid for them, not knowing that in London nobody cared if you were a Catholic married to a Protestant. As far as they could see nobody cared here anyway. You could be writhing in agony half the night and no one would even come to see if you were being murdered. At home in Belfast people cared too much in some ways. They could never let you be. Kevin said that his father certainly would not wish them well. He would take it as an insult to himself, his family, and his religion. Kevin had betrayed them.

They ate at the little card-table with the torn green baize top. Most things provided with the room were torn or broken or damaged in some way or other. They ate quickly, enjoying the hot tasty food, mopping the egg from their plates with slices of bread taken from the packet that sat between them on the table.

'Nothing to beat it,' said Kevin, sighing contentedly. 'Bacon and eggs!'

They drank their tea from bright red mugs. Sadie loved the vivid colour: it warmed her and made her forget the dreariness of the room. All the splashes of colour in the room belonged to them, the lime green sheets, canary yellow blankets, red-handled saucepans, pale blue plates, purple towels, and Sadie's latest purchase, which she had been quite unable to resist, a soft, furry, scarlet rug. She had brought the rug home from the shop where she worked, hugging it close to her, excited by the idea of having it on the floor of their room where she would see it each morning when she opened her eyes. She had spread it out before Kevin who had admired it cautiously and then asked the price. It had cost more than they could afford, and she had taken it on hire purchase. They had enough on hire purchase, said Kevin, too much in fact, what with weekly payments to various clubs. They had come to London without possessions, Sadie even without clothes, and so, being forced to buy the basic necessities, they had bought on credit and were paying back weekly. Bright colours cost only a little more than plain, Sadie had pleaded, and Kevin had sighed and said, 'Oh, all right then,' unable himself to resist Sadie's enthusiasm. But the weekly payments had grown until now they were a sizable sum and Kevin said they must buy nothing more until these debts were cleared. Sadie agreed. She did not mean to be extravagant. It was just that sometimes she saw things . . .

Money was tight. Sadie did not earn very much, travelling was expensive, and Kevin's work as a labourer was casual so that sometimes he had a week between jobs. He did not much like working as a labourer, and would have preferred a job where he could use the skill in his hands, rather than the strength. Work on the building sites cut his hands, bruised them and toughened them, thickening the pads of his fingers, breaking the nails. But in spite of that, his fingers were nimble, and he could take apart old wireless sets and reassemble them with amazing speed.

'Where'll we go the day?' said Kevin. 'I'll get the map.'

He spread it on the floor and they crouched over it. They were working their way round London, covering it systematically, area by area. In the beginning, when they had gone to all the famous places like Piccadilly and Hyde Park, Sadie had been thrilled just to stand in the streets and gaze. 'Regent Street,' she would say, shaking her head with disbelief. 'Can you get over it, Kev? We're really here.' She liked London at week-ends when they went exploring, but weekdays she hated when they went to work, pushing and shoving with the crowds in the morning, coming back pushing and shoving with the crowds in the evening, to return to the cold grey room to fry fish fingers on the smelly ring and then sit afterwards with the dark closing in on the street outside.

'What about Kensington?' suggested Kevin, stabbing the map with his finger. 'We've never been there.'

'Kensington?'

'It's a posh district.'

'That's for us then.' Sadie jumped up.

Kevin washed the dishes whilst she dressed herself. She pulled on jeans and a sweater and tied her long fair hair back in a pony tail.

'You don't look any different from when I first met you,' said Kevin. 'Four years ago!'

'I was only thirteen then.' Sadie flicked her pony tail. 'I thought I was looking mature these days.'

'Oh aye, like an ould married wumman of two months standing! What'll you be like after two years? Or twenty?'

They laughed and she put her hand into his. There were times when she found if difficult to believe that she really was married. Often when she woke in the morning she found that she had forgotten. She would turn to see his dark head on the

pillow and would feel strange for a moment but as soon as
he opened his eyes and smiled at her the strangeness went and
it felt right to be married and living with him.

Kevin opened the door and they went out into the streets of
London together.

Chapter Two

'I really fancied that house in the square,' said Sadie. 'The one with the black iron balcony. And the fancy car parked outside.'

'You did, did you?' said Kevin. 'Should get it for a cool fifty thousand.'

'Fifty thousand! You're jokin'!'

''Deed I'm not. This is a fancy city, Sadie. And the prices are fancy to go with it.'

Sadie sighed. They would just have to start doing the football pools. Her father had done them every week for as long as she could remember; he would sit on a Thursday night at the kitchen table in his shirt sleeves filling in the coupon, licking the end of his pencil, frowning with concentration, and nobody would dare interrupt him until he said, 'There, that's done, you never know your luck,' and laid down his pencil. Once he had won five pounds. Her mother had taken three of them, tucking the notes firmly into the pocket of her apron, and the rest her father had spent in the pub. It seemed a lifetime away, but she supposed, on a Thursday, her father would still be filling in his coupon.

She nestled her head against Kevin's shoulder, he tightened his arm round her waist. They were tired, their feet were slow, for they had walked for hours, until Sadie had grown a blister on her heel. The daylight was going, the air was cool and lights were springing up stabbing the grey dusk. Now they would go home, she would make tea, and they they would sit and talk about the day when they would be rich. They wanted to travel the world, have children, and own a house.

As they turned the corner into their own street they were almost knocked over by two boys fighting. One was white, the other black. Many immigrants lived in the area. Sadie and Kevin had never seen so many brown skins before they came to London.

'What's going on then?' Kevin seized both of the boys by their collars.

'Lay off!' The white boy kicked Kevin on the shin. Kevin took him by the shoulders and held him fast.

'Less of that, young fella!'

'Dirty ould Mick!' The boy stuck out his tongue.

Sadie laughed. 'Dear love us, I never thought I'd hear that in these parts. He must have seen you going into the church, Kevin.'

Kevin smiled too. But he kept hold of the wriggling boy. The black boy stood a yard away, his large dark eyes watching carefully.

'I'm stronger than you, boy,' said Kevin. 'And don't you forget it.' He had fought often as a child and beaten most of the lads in his district, and then had come a time when fighting had sickened him.

'Let go of him, mister,' said the black boy, and suddenly he lashed out with a foot catching Kevin on the ankle.

Kevin winced but did not release the other boy.

'Watch it!' said Sadie. She felt as if she was back in Belfast again, involved in the life of the street. 'Is he a friend of yours then?' she asked, nodding at the boy Kevin held.

'Sort of.'

Kevin pushed the boy away from him. 'Away ye go!'

The two boys scampered across the street. When they reached the other pavement they stopped and turned. 'Dirty ould Micks!' they called together.

Sadie and Kevin laughed, joined hands again.

'First time I've been called a Mick,' said Sadie. She looked up at Kevin and saw that he was looking serious. 'You weren't bothered by them were you?'

'Course not. No, I was thinking of something else. It's something I have to ask you.'

'To do with being Mick?'

'Yes, well in a way.' Kevin cleared his throat. 'You're not going to like what I say –'

'Don't say it then,' she put in quickly. 'Sure we've had a lovely day and we don't want it spoiled.'

Kevin sighed.

They walked the rest of the way along the street in silence. There were a few people about but no one spoke to them. Sadie had tried saying good morning to one or two of the women but they had looked at her suspiciously, watched her closely till she was out of sight but had said nothing. People were poor in this street and their poverty made them suspicious. They lived in close huddles, strangers in the city; they heard one another breathe through walls and fight with husbands and wives but they did not communicate with them, unless they were of the same family or race. At one end of the street lived a dozen or so West Indians. They herded together, held parties, made noises till late in the night. Sometimes when she heard them Sadie would wish that they would ask them to come and join them. She liked the sound of their singing. She missed people. She had always known everyone in her street, in her district, had stopped to chat, exchange gossip, commiserate over the bad news, rejoice over the good.

An Indian woman was leaning against the railings of the house next to theirs. She wore a sari, deep purple with a gold border, and she held a baby in her arms. As they drew level with her Sadie looked at her and smiled. The woman's face did not move but her eyes seemed to soften.

Sadie took a step nearer to look at the baby. 'What a lovely baby!' she said.

The woman smiled.

Sadie put out her finger and touched the baby's fat brown hand. He hesitated for a moment, eyeing Sadie's finger with his large black eyes and then he grabbed it and pulled it towards his mouth.

'He is cutting teeth,' said the woman in very good English. 'Poor wee fellow!'

'Lara!' a voice called from the house, a man's voice.

'I must go,' said the Indian woman.

Sadie withdrew her finger from the baby's hand. His mouth drooped petulantly making both Sadie and his mother laugh.

'Lara!' called the voice again.

'Good-bye,' said Sadie.

'Good-bye,' said Lara. She gathered the edge of her sari in one hand and took the baby into the house. He watched Sadie over his mother's shoulder. She waved to him.

'I think perhaps I've made a friend,' said Sadie triumphantly.

'Two friends,' said Kevin.

'Yes. Two friends.'

They went into their house. The entrance hall smelt of cat and boiled cabbage, though they had almost ceased to notice it now. Kevin took the key from his pocket and put it in the lock.

'It's not locked,' he said in surprise.

'Must have forgotten to lock it. Now that I come to think of it I don't remember you doing it.'

Kevin put his hand round the corner and fumbled for the light switch. The light went on, and he stepped back in astonishment.

'What's up?' said Sadie, coming in behind him; then she too stood still and gazed at the room. It had been turned upside down.

The drawers were open, and the cupboard door. Clothes were spread across the room, all their possessions had been pulled out and raked over.

'What would anyone have against us here?' said Sadie. 'If it'd been at home –'

'We'd have had a bomb through our window if we'd been in Belfast. But I don't like the look of this at all.' Kevin knelt down to pick up some of the things. 'No one knows anything about us here. I think someone's been in to see what they can steal.'

'Steal? We've nothing worth stealing.' Sadie shook her head with disbelief.

'No one round here's got very much. Depends what you have before you think anything's worth stealing. Let's see if anything's missing.'

A number of things were missing: their bright red mugs, the furry rug, a purple tray with pink flowers painted on it that Sadie had coveted for two weeks and bought only on Friday, when she had got her pay. She exploded.

'Of all the mean, nasty –!'

'They've taken our cutlery too,' said Kevin grimly.

'And the butter and cheese has gone. What kind of monsters can they be?' wailed Sadie.

Some of their clothes had also gone, the better ones, so that all they had left were the old ones they wore at week-ends.

'I've nothing to go to my work in,' wailed Sadie. 'I can't go in jeans.'

She raged and stormed; Kevin sat quietly on the floor, his face dark and brooding.

'We should have locked the door of course.' He sighed, stood up. 'We'd better go and have a word with old Crackers.'

Mrs Kyrakis's door was closed and not a sound was to be heard behind it. Kevin knocked twice calling her name.

'Sleeping,' said Sadie loudly. 'What an eejit!'

Kevin knocked again, several times. A woman came past, her feet slopping along the linoleum in felt slippers. She was a thin woman who went up and down the street in an overall and slippers every day, her hair in rollers. She reminded Sadie of the women in her street in Belfast.

'She'll not answer,' the woman said. 'The place could go up in flames and she'd not pay any attention.'

'I'll break the door down if I have to,' said Kevin.

But the woman had already gone, not interested any further. She had dead eyes, thought Sadie. She shivered.

'Mrs Kyrakis,' said Kevin in a determined voice, 'our room has been burgled and we would like a word with you. If you don't open up we'll have to call the police.'

He knew he would not call the police, and so would she. If he did call them they would pay no attention anyway, and even if they did and they came, they would look round the house and shake their heads. They had plenty of other things to occupy themselves with. Two red mugs and a tin tray and some cheap clothes . . .

'Mrs Kyrakis,' shouted Sadie desperately. 'For dear sake, can you not hear us?'

A West African came into the hall and went up the stairs. He looked over the banisters at them.

'This place is like a looney bin,' said Sadie. She leant back against the wall and folded her arms. 'I'm stopping here till she comes out. She'll need to go to the loo sometime.'

Kevin laughed. 'I've seen that stubborn look on your face before!'

The door opened suddenly, making them jump. Mrs Kyrakis stood there with the light behind her, holding a shawl round her shoulders.

'What the devil you make that noise for?' she demanded.

A sweet, suffocating smell emanated from the open doorway.

'Our room's been burgled,' said Kevin. 'And half our things taken.'

'There must be a thief in the house,' said Sadie.

The landlady shrugged. 'What you want me to do about it?'

'Come and see,' said Sadie.

Mrs Kyrakis pulled her own door shut and followed them

up the passage. She stood at the door of the room, looked round briefly, then shrugged again.

'What you expect me to do? Fourteen people live in this house.'

'If we searched the rooms we'd probably find our stuff,' said Sadie.

'Search?' said Mrs Kyrakis with amazement.

Sadie's shoulders slumped. Of course they couldn't search the rooms. The inhabitants would never let them.

'Sorry we bothered you,' said Kevin sarcastically, but his sarcasm was wasted on Mrs Kyrakis.

'Keep the door locked,' she said. 'Less bother that way.'

She went back down the passage to her own room. They shut the door. Sadie sat down on the bed and thumped her fist on the eiderdown.

'Rotten, stinking, miserable –' She could not go on, she was crying. She seldom cried and the tears took her by surprise. She wiped her eyes with the back of her hand. She felt Kevin's arm round her shoulder.

'Never mind, love,' he said softly. 'We'll get over it. Sure, haven't we got over worse?'

'But we've not got much.'

'We've still one another. Isn't that the main thing?'

She stopped crying. She smiled at him. He was warm and solid and no one could take him away from her.

'Course it's the main thing. But if I ever get my hands on the hallions that did it –!'

Kevin laughed. 'You're a devil when you're worked up. That was what I first liked in you.'

They tidied the room, and to make herself feel better Sadie scrubbed the floor and cleaned the window. After that they sat in front of the one-bar electric fire scorching their ankles and discussed how they would furnish the house they had liked in the square in Kensington, the one that Kevin thought would cost fifty thousand pounds.

Chapter Three

Early morning cold. Sadie shivered and wriggled her shoulders inside her old red dressing gown, glad at least that the thief had not taken that. It was old, of course, and had a hole that she had always meant to darn in one elbow. She had been given the dressing gown for her thirteenth birthday. She smiled when she thought of that for she had never expected to be wearing it when she was a married woman. She had fancied that she would be slinking around in a long filmy negligee. She giggled.

'What's the big joke?' demanded Kevin, lifting the electric razor off his chin.

'Nothing,' said Sadie. 'Oh, just us. This room, and all.'

'You'd better be getting on with my lunch or I'll be late.'

Kevin continued shaving, Sadie spread slices of bread with margarine and wondered what else to put on them since the cheese had been taken.

'It'll have to be jam,' she said.

'O.K'.

He did not mind as long as it was food and there was enough to fill his stomach. Working outside made him ravenous. When he had finished shaving he pulled on a heavy sweater and combed his thick dark hair. Before he went out he sat down in front of the electric fire to have a last heat, spreading out his hands, holding them close to the red bar. Sadie put the sandwiches into a plastic lunch box, added a wrinkled apple. and filled his flask with hot sweetened tea. He was ready to go.

He took his jacket from behind the door, slung it round his

shoulders, lifted his lunch box and flask. She put her arms round his neck and rubbed her cheek against his. He kissed her.

'Must go, love.'

She nodded.

She went to the window, drew back the curtain. On his way past he stopped and leaned his nose against the window, flattening it, making her laugh. She put her nose against the window too, so that it met his through the glass. Then he straightened his back, blew her a kiss and was gone, striding across the road, whistling, his jacket hooked over his shoulder on one finger. He seldom felt the cold and she often nagged him for not wearing his jacket. Whenever she nagged him she could hear her mother's voice behind her like an echo. When she thought of being like her mother she was horrified.

For a moment after he had gone she felt lonely. The street was still dark. A few men were on their way to work, one or two were coming back after night-shift. She closed the curtain, turning back into the room. The light was on, it might as well have been night. She did not have to go out for another hour. The warm bed tempted her, but if she did go back, getting up the second time would be all the harder and she might be tempted to lie in and not go to work at all. She did not like her work; it was boring. But so was Kevin's, and they needed the money.

She washed and dressed, putting on jeans and a sweater. She would leave early and buy herself a cheap dress in the shop. Now she felt better. There was a new day ahead and who knew what might come of it? She sang to herself while she washed the dishes and made the bed. As she tidied the room she wondered at herself for there was a time when anything remotely domesticated sickened her, but she wanted to make this room as nice as she could for Kevin and herself. 'You're the absolute end, Sadie Jackson,' her mother used to say. 'You could stir your room with a stick.'

Sitting on the edge of the bed, Sadie thought about her mother and father and brother Tommy. Every day the news about Ulster was bad and every day she half-expected a telegram. She would know what was in it before she opened it. Whenever she read of a bomb in a pub or a shop she would think her mother might have been shopping, or her father could have been having a pint of Guinness with his friend Mr Mullet on their way home from a Lodge meeting. She supposed he still went to his Lodge meetings; Orange Lodge meetings, where the Brethren pledged themselves to defend the Protestant faith. And Kevin's family lived in a Catholic area, a stronghold of the IRA. His younger sisters and brothers roamed the streets playing at terrorists killing British soldiers. Yes, she and Kevin were well out of it.

It was light when she set off. She walked quickly to the Underground station to join the crowds of snuffling, frowning, irritated people on their way to work. When she travelled on the Underground she thought what a terrible waste of energy it was, that people must wear themselves out before they were old doing this every day, and that their lungs must rot breathing in the filthy air and smoke.

She squeezed herself on to a train, the door barely managing to close behind her. She had to stand of course and this morning could not even reach a strap to hold on to. Strap-hanging she rather liked, swaying with the movement of the train. Her back was pressed against the door, her nose rested against the coat of the man in front who seemed oblivious of his surroundings and was reading a newspaper. She squinted over his shoulder. BOMB EXPLOSION IN BELFAST said the headline, leaping out from the paper to hit her in the eye. FIVE KILLED TEN INJURED. Her heart beat faster, she felt sickness rise from her stomach to her throat. She stood on tiptoe craning her head to read a bit more of the report. It was not in her area, or in Kevin's. It was probably all right. It was strange: in a way she worried more about the bombs and shootings here than she had done in Belfast. There, they had lived with them, accepting them as part of everyday life; here, after only a few weeks away from it all, it seemed fantastic to expect to live with such horror every day. And you worried more about people when you couldn't see them.

She almost missed her station, having to jump off quickly at the last moment. She had to change trains and the next one was just as crowded. Two girls beside her were moaning about it being Monday morning. They looked half-asleep and must have put on their eye make-up in a hurry for it was blurred and smeared. The girls at Sadie's work dressed themselves up as if they were going to a party and were never seen with their faces bare. They made fun of her behind her back for not being 'with-it'. She knew, but did not care particularly. She called them 'eejits' under her breath. She had something much better than they did: Kevin. She smiled, forgetting the girls and the crowded train, and was still thinking about him and the way his hair curled round his neck when she reached her station. Again she jumped off at the last minute. Up the escalator she went, following the crowd, and surfaced into the outside world again.

She was the first of the girls to arrive at the store. It was not a large store and not what was known as a 'high-class' shop. The supervisor was there in her shiny black dress and back-combed hair. Sadie never liked supervisors. She had had experience of them before, and department heads. The ones she had encountered were soured women fed up with life, hating to see anyone else enjoying it. Sadie did and usually showed it.

'Well!' Miss Cullen ran her eye down Sadie's jeans. 'You can't serve behind a counter in those trousers.'

'No, I know. But we had burglars last night ...' Sadie launched into a long story giving full details, but Miss Cullen was not interested. There was new stock to be unpacked and she had a headache. It was a typical Monday morning.

'You simply cannot wear jeans in the store,' she snapped,

pinching her mouth so that the skin puckered all round it.

'I thought maybe I could buy myself a dress and pay it off Saturday's wages . . .'

'All right, all right.' Miss Cullen cut her off. She put her hand to her head. 'But you'd better wait till Miss Robson comes in.'

She went away muttering, shaking her head. Sadie went to the cloakroom to wait for Daphne Robson who was in charge of the dress department. Daphne was for ever changing her wardrobe; she was reputed to have thirty pairs of shoes, she wore false eyelashes so long and thick that Sadie wondered if she could see through them, and she talked endlessly of clothes and men. As far as Sadie could make out she had nearly as many men as she had shoes.

Several other girls arrived and passed remarks about Sadie's jeans.

'New outfit huh? Real cool!'

'Mucking out the barn today are you, ducks?'

And there were lots of giggles.

'Fancied a change,' said Sadie airily. 'Jeans are dead comfy.'

'Miss Cullen'll give you dead comfy!'

The girls turned their backs on her and began to chat to one another, recounting stories of Saturday night and new boys met and old ones dismissed. Sadie had not managed to make a friend here. This puzzled her for she had never had trouble making friends before. Usually she found it easy to talk to people. It was probably because she was married, she thought. Most of the girls were single, they went around together, shared secrets. Two of them were married but they were older than Sadie and kept to themselves, exchanging notes of recipes or where to get cheap blankets, and at lunchtime they shopped together.

Daphne Robson took Sadie along to the dress department, making it quite clear that Sadie was a nuisance, that otherwise Daphne could have had a last cigarette before she started work.

'There you are, take your pick,' she said, unlocking the showcases.

Sadie looked through the dresses. Daphne leant against the counter yawning.

'Don't take all day,' she said.

Sadie thought they were all terrible. 'Can't see anything I like.'

Daphne shrugged. 'Maybe you should look in the kids' department. Might be more in your line.'

'There's no need to be snarky,' said Sadie clearly.

'What'd you say?' Daphne stopped looking bored and stood up straight.

'I said you didn't have to be snarky. I'm not a kid.'

'Are you not?' said Daphne, trying to imitate Sadie's accent. 'You're damned cheeky though. You'd better get along out of here.' She was angry now.

'I'm choosing a dress first,' said Sadie, standing her ground.

'I'll report you to Miss Cullen.'

'For what? Offending you? Who the hell do you think you are?' Sadie's cheeks were hot, her temper was rising. 'You think you're the bees' knees just because you've eyelashes on you that you could sweep the streets with and you mince around as if you was a model! If you want the truth, you're a right looking sight!'

For a moment Sadie thought Daphne Robson was going to strike her. She knew she had gone too far. It was one of her faults. But she got carried away when she was stirred up.

Daphne Robson stalked off. Sadie took the least offensive dress from the rail. It was her size and the colour was not too bad, dark orange. She carried it back to the cloakroom where Daphne was in full spate telling the girls of Sadie's impudence. One or two of the girls were giggling for Daphne Robson was not as popular as she liked to think, and many were bored with the tales of the thirty pairs of shoes and men, all of whom were more handsome and more desirable than anything anyone else could hope to aspire to.

Sadie took off her jeans, put on the orange dress. She brushed out her hair in front of the mirror. She did not even glance at any of the others.

'No wonder they're shooting one another to pieces where she comes from,' said Daphne. 'If she's anything to go by!'

'Come on now, girls,' said Miss Cullen, fussing into the room. 'Time you were at your counters. The doors will be opening in five minutes.'

The girls lifted their handbags, dispersed to their departments. Sadie was on the haberdashery counter with an elderly woman who had been serving cards of elastic and reels of thread for forty years. She told this to Sadie every day with pride. Sadie found cards of elastic and hooks and eyes most uninteresting though the reels of thread were better. The colours pleased her, trays of different colours shading from the very lightest to the darkest until the thread almost turned black.

Business was slack on a Monday morning. Most of the time they stood behind the counter and yawned. Miss Marshall did not have much to say apart from referring to her experience in haberdashery and whenever Sadie brought up another topic she would look at her with mild blue eyes and say nothing in return. She herself moved forward to serve every customer and Sadie was only permitted to serve when Miss Marshall was otherwise engaged. Except for Saturdays, when the store was crowded and people were impatient, they did not really need two on the counter.

Sadie stood with her back against the wall and thought about old friends and neighbours. There were some she longed to see and find out what was happening to them. She would even like to see Linda Mullet, her old friend and enemy, with whom she had gone to school and played in the street. Linda, with her wiggly walk and her pert way of holding her head, and her mother with her fizzy blonde hair and steep-heeled shoes lounging against the door jamb smoking a fag ... 'How're you the day, Sadie?' she would say, hoping for scandal.

Sadie loved to give it to her. Mrs Mullet had plenty to keep her going now. 'Fancy Sadie Jackson getting married to a Mick! Mind you, I always said she'd come to no good.' Sadie grinned. If Linda and Mrs Mullet were to come walking across the floor now, she would leap over the counter to meet them, like the winners at Wimbledon did when they were carried away by excitement. That was what got her down here: there was never a chance of meeting someone you knew unexpectedly. She walked always amongst strangers.

By lunchtime Sadie had sold one zip fastener and a reel of white thread.

'Couldn't say I've earned my keep,' she said to Miss Marshall as she lifted her handbag.

Miss Marshall said nothing.

Sadie sat in the cloakroom to eat her sandwiches. The other girls went out to cafés round about but she could not afford to spend the money. When she had eaten she went round the shops buying a few groceries and choosing things in shop windows that she would buy one day. After lunch she released Miss Marshall and for one hour Sadie was alone behind the counter. That was the hour of the day she liked best.

The shop closed at half-past five. By then she was tired even though she had not done much work. All the hanging around with nothing to do was more tiring than working hard.

When she came into the cloakroom at the end of the day, three or four girls who were talking together stopped and looked round at her.

'Hi!' said Rita, who worked on shoes.

'Hi!' said Sadie.

'Have you a minute?'

Sadie went over to them.

'We were wondering if you were free this evening?' said

Rita. 'You see, we're having a night out, a few of us. And we thought maybe you'd like to come.'

'Oh I would,' said Sadie at once, but her enthusiasm died quickly as she remembered Kevin. 'But I can't. You see, my husband –'

Rita nodded. 'We didn't know if he'd mind or not.'

'He would,' said Sadie. 'But thanks a lot for asking me.'

'Come another time.'

'All right.' Sadie nodded. She took her coat down from the peg, happy that they had asked her, sad that she could not go. She longed to go out for an evening with a bunch of girls and have a good laugh. She and Kevin were together on their own all the time and sometimes she felt bored. The thought appalled her. She bit her lip. But she loved Kevin. Of course he didn't bore her. You couldn't be bored by someone you loved. Or could you? There were still a lot of things she was not sure of.

'Good night, Sadie,' called Rita.

'Good night,' called the other girls with her.

'Good night,' said Sadie. 'Have a good time.'

They went out chattering and laughing, full of the joys of the evening ahead. The cloakroom was quiet now. Sadie thought of going home to the dingy room to fry sausages on the gas ring and then to sit in front of the fire talking about things they could never have. She wanted to go dancing and laugh and talk with lots of people. She didn't want to sit every evening in a room with one man, even though she loved him.

She walked slowly to the tube station. A train was leaving the platform as she got in and she had to wait a while for the next one. It was packed. The passengers looked tired and hungry and unhealthy, their faces were fawn-coloured and their eyes red-rimmed. Someone stood right in the middle of Sadie's foot and did not even turn round to apologize. She made a face at his back. Her foot would probably be bruised for a week.

She hobbled out of the station remembering the sound of

the girls' laughter; she thought of them chattering and enjoying themselves. Suddenly she realized that she had left the shopping in the cloakroom. Kevin would be waiting for her to bring in food and cook it for him. He would be there now, starving, wondering what was keeping her, his brow creased with irritation because she was late. Why shouldn't she be late if she wanted to? Why should he expect to sit there waiting to be fed? Standing there in that cold foreign street she wished she was free to do what she wanted. She hated being married. And she hated London. She wanted to go home to Belfast, bombs and all.

Chapter Four

At lunch-time Kevin sat on a wall by the side of the road eating his sandwiches. In front of him the strip of road was open, dug up by drills and picks that now lay idle. The other men had gone to the pub. They usually did in the middle of the day, and often at the end too. Digging up roads was thirsty work. Occasionally Kevin went with them for a pint of beer but he could not afford to do it very often, nor did he want to particularly. He took quite a bit of teasing from the men.

'You're the brave boy getting yourself tied to a woman at your age!'

Most of the men were Irish and Catholics like himself, but from the South. They had left home, not because of bombs and trouble but because they couldn't find work at home. Many had left families there to whom they sent money every week. They were rough, tough men, ready to fight. Kevin had known many like them before. He remembered a neighbour, Pat Rafferty, a big hulk of a man, with hands like hams held ready to fight at the slightest provocation. So Kevin found the men familiar and could hold his ground with them but found no one amongst them whom he would want to have as a friend. To start with they all drank too much and on Friday, pay night, went straight to the pub, scoffing at him for hurrying home to give his pay packet to his wife.

But Kevin was not thinking of the men now or their drinking habits. He was thinking of what the foreman had told him this morning: he was to be laid off on Friday along with two others. There wasn't enough work. The words had brought sickness to the pit of Kevin's stomach.

He had been out of work before, in Belfast, and knew what it did to you to have long idle days with nothing to do and no money to collect at the end of the week. The foreman had said Kevin would be sure to find something else if he went along to the Labour Exchange. He would probably get another casual labouring job and that would last a week or two or maybe more and then he would be back again at the Exchange looking for something else. He was sick of this way of living, doing casual work that meant nothing except for the money you collected at the end of the week. He couldn't see himself going on like that for ever. He didn't want to be digging holes in the road when he was forty.

He finished the sandwiches, ate the wrinkled apple and wondered how Sadie was getting on. In the evening she would tell him about the other girls and make him laugh. They sounded like a real bunch of eejits. He uncorked the thermos, poured the scalding tea into the top and drank, enjoying the warmth of the liquid flowing down through his body. It was a cold day to sit on a wall and eat lunch, even for him. He had put on his jacket, which would have pleased Sadie.

The last drop of tea gone, he stood up, stretched himself and began to walk. He looked at the faces of the people as he passed. People did not seem to really look at one another here. They were not interested. They were too busy hurrying. What for, he wondered? When he walked streets he was used to the sight of known faces and now he missed them. He shook his head ruefully. He was feeling homesick today, longing for a sight of his mother or sister Brede. At his age!

He bought a newspaper and leant against a corner to read it. FIVE DEAD TEN INJURED; the headline was the first thing his eye hit on. He read the report carefully, looking for the names of the victims. No one he knew. He sighed with relief. One day there was bound to be someone. It was getting worse and he did not see how it could even start to get better. And yet he longed to be there, for it was not all bombs and blood and suffering. People laughed a lot and enjoyed themselves, when they were allowed to, and they were friendly. They were certainly not friendly in London and he knew it was getting on Sadie's nerves.

He folded the paper, put it in his jacket pocket and walked back to the site. All afternoon he worked with a juddering electric drill, standing in a narrow trench. As he worked he though about the pleasant things of Ireland, the green glens of Antrim, the Atlantic rollers breaking on the white sands of Portrush, the sea whipping round the rocks at Bangor in County Down. He and Sadie had spent many good days in the country and at the seaside. Here they found it difficult to get out into real country. It took a long time and cost a lot of money.

'Hey, Kev!' yelled the man next to him in the trench. 'Wake up there! Knocking off time.'

Kevin put aside the drill.

'Don't want to work overtime,' said Dave. 'Not unless they're paying you. You were far away by the looks of it.'

'I was thinking about . . . about Ireland.'

'That place! Devil a place that it is. It gets into your blood. You can't stand it when you're there and you can't get it out of your mind when you're not.'

Kevin smiled. Dave was all right. He had hard calloused hands and a face like leather that had come from working as a labourer in London for twenty years. He still talked about going home for good even though everyone knew that he never would.

Kevin went to the Labour Exchange before going home. He said that he would dearly like to try something different.

'Could I start as an apprentice in a trade?' he asked, though even as he said it he wondered how they would be able to manage on the small wage. But he did not have to worry about that for even if he could have survived on the money he was not allowed to try. He was too old.

'Too old?' he repeated. 'I'm only nineteen.'

'You have to start before.'

'I see. Oh well . . .'

The woman said she would see what work there was going next week in labouring. If he would call back on Friday . . .?

Ah well, at least it was work, he reminded himself. When he had been out of work in Belfast he had had to live off his family.

He walked all the way home. It was nearly three miles but he did not mind for he was not in a hurry. Sadie did not come back till after he did and he hated going into the cold empty room to sit and wait for her.

But he was back before her in spite of the delay at the Labour Exchange and the walk. It was grey dusk in the room and the chill seemed worse than the street. He put on the light and the electric fire, and set the kettle to boil. Then he turned to the letter with the Belfast postmark that he had found on the hall table. It was from Brede. He ripped open the envelope.

Their mother was ill and was to go into hospital for an operation. 'Nothing to worry about,' wrote Brede, who would write that no matter what the trouble was.

'Just a routine operation, the doctor says, but I thought I should let you know. I am taking time off work to look after the family.' Brede had often looked after the family, every time her mother had gone into hospital to have another baby. Kevin bit his lip. How bad was she? He would write tonight to his father and ask to be told the truth.

He glanced at the clock. Where on earth was Sadie? He was too restless to sit; he got up, went out again and walked back down the road to the Underground station. He watched the crowds pouring out but did not find Sadie amongst them. She might have got off at a different station, a little further away, just to make a change. She did that sometimes, for she hated getting in a rut and doing the same thing day after day. He returned home but the room was still empty and quiet. The single bar of fire glowed, a wisp of steam escaped from the kettle spout, nothing else in the room moved. He boiled the kettle up again and made a pot of tea, leaving the curtains open so that Sadie would see the light shining out as she came up the street.

As he drank his tea he reread Brede's letter, searching for any shred of extra information between the lines. But there it was, the bald fact that his mother was ill and was going into hospital to have an operation. And he was hundreds of miles away, not even able to go and visit her. He thought of Brede bearing it all alone, except for their father. She would look after the other seven children, feed them and scold them and worry about them when they were not home by dark, and she would go up to the hospital to reassure their mother that everyone was all right.

He poured more tea. He held up the cup to the light: there was a crack in the side clogged with grime and through it tea trickled in small droplets. He made a face at it. He had meant to buy two new mugs on his way home tonight, bright yellow ones that he had noticed in a window, but with thoughts of his job whirling in his head he had quite forgotten. Sadie would like the yellow. Two yellow mugs sitting on the table would be like two splashes of sunshine in the room. 'We'll have to make our own sunshine,' Sadie had said when they had first seen the room on a grey, rainy day.

Where the devil was she? His stomach rumbled with hunger. He looked at the clock again: She should have been back nearly an hour ago.

Chapter Five

'Where on earth have you been?' Kevin demanded, as Sadie came into the room.

'What do you mean – where have I been? At work of course. Where do you think I've been? Out enjoying myself?' Her eyes flared with annoyance.

'But you're near on an hour late. I've been sitting waiting on you.'

'Too bad isn't it?' She flung herself down in a chair without taking off her coat. 'I suppose you've been sitting here waiting for me to come back and make your tea.'

'Well, I'm hungry. I've been working all day.'

'So have I. And I'm hungry and all. Why should I have to come back and cook your tea while you sit and twiddle your thumbs? You never think to cook mine.'

'But the woman usually does the cooking.'

'She does, does she? Well, I don't see why she should. Not if she's working all day and gets in after the man.'

Kevin looked at her but she would not look at him. She glanced around the room, her mouth set in a hard line that he had not seen on her before.

'If you'd wanted me to do it you could have asked me,' he said.

'You might have thought to offer,' she said.

Feet clattered overhead making their ceiling shake. Sadie looked up.

'I hate this place,' she said.

'We can't afford anything else and you know it.'

'Oh, I know it all right.'

'Want a cup of tea?'

She shrugged. He poured her one and she took it, still without looking at him.

'What's the matter with you?' he asked.

'Nothing. I'm just fed up.'

'Fed up?'

She looked now. 'Yes, fed up. Fed up working and not being able to buy myself any decent clothes or go out at night and have any fun. It's like being a prisoner shut in this box.'

'It's the same for me, Sadie,' he said in a low voice.

'I'm not saying it isn't.'

He tipped the teapot up. It was bone-dry. He refilled the kettle. He might as well have another cup of tea at least. It didn't look as if he was going to get any food.

'Are you saying you wish you hadn't got married?'

'I never said that at all,' she snapped.

'That's what you seemed to be saying.'

She did not like the sound of his voice. When it was low and well controlled it meant he was angry underneath, getting ready to boil up and lash out, and when he was angry his eyes were black and dangerous and she felt a little afraid of him. She wriggled, undid the top button of her coat.

'Don't tell me you're staying,' he said sarcastically.

'I wouldn't if I didn't have to,' she answered, her temper rising too now. She wondered how she had ever thought he loved her. She wished she never had to set eyes on him again.

'If that's the case I can soon leave myself,' he said, lifting his jacket.

'Where are you going?' she asked, alarmed.

'Out. To the pub. Or wherever I fancy. And maybe I'll find myself a girl with a sweeter tongue on her than you. I'm not staying here to be spoken to like dirt.' He went to the door.

'Don't, Kevin!' she cried.

He turned back and stood looking at her.

'I'm sorry,' she said. 'I never meant it.'

He took a step towards her, she rose out of her chair to meet him. They put their arms round each other's necks and hugged one another. Sadie was laughing and crying at the same time.

'Course I want to be married to you, Kev. I don't know what gets into me at times. I say the wildest things. Oh, but we're like a couple of kids fighting still!'

'It's all right,' he said. 'I was just worried about you being late. I was thinking of you under a bus –' He stroked her hair.

'You needn't worry. I'll never fall under a bus.' She wrinkled her nose at him and he laughed. 'It'd need to be some bus that'd get me.'

'What was up with you then when you came in the door?'

She told him about the girls at work, how she had envied them going out all dressed up to have a night out. 'But I don't envy them really, Kevin. I'd rather come home to you.'

'Good.' He released her. 'I tell you what. If you give me the food I'll cook it for you tonight. I can't promise not to burn it, mind, but I'll do my best.'

Her smile faded. 'Well . . . to tell the truth love, I left it at the shop.'

'You left it! For heaven's sake, Sadie, you're an absolute twit!'

'You've no call to say that to me. Anyone can forget a thing once in a while.' She stopped and shook her head. 'Oh, don't let's start up arguing again. We're devils for it. I'll go down to the Indian shop and get us some fish fingers. You could set the table and make some toast for us.'

'O.K. I'll burn my fingers for your sake!'

She ran along the street feeling happy again. It had been stupid of her to think that Rita and her friends were better off than she was. Kevin was the best boy in the whole world and she was lucky to be with him.

The Indian shop was busy. It was self-service and open till

late at night. People often stopped on their way home from work to buy their groceries. Sadie pushed her way round with the wire basket buying two or three things, unable to afford very much with the prospect of the dress to pay for. In front of the deep freeze she came upon Lara.

'Hello,' said Sadie.

'Hello.' Lara smiled. She had a beautiful smile, wide and serene.

'I left the sausages at work,' said Sadie, taking a packet of fish fingers from the fridge.

Lara laughed. 'Your husband would not like that.'

'He didn't.' Sadie made a face. 'But he's recovered.' She hesitated, then said, 'I was wondering if you'd like to come in and have a cup of coffee sometime. Wednesday afternoon. It's my half-day. You could bring the baby.'

Lara hesitated too before she spoke. 'That would be nice. Thank you. I will try.'

'Good.'

Sadie ran all the way home again and arrived with her cheeks flushed pink. A smell of scorching met her.

'It's no easy business making toast on a bar like this,' said Kevin.

'Never mind,' she cried gaily. 'I like burnt toast.'

As she put down the fish fingers she noticed the letter on the table. 'From Brede?'

Kevin nodded. 'My mother's ill. She's to have an operation.'

'Oh Kevin! I'm sorry.'

'I wish I was nearer,' he sighed.

Sadie put the fish fingers on to fry, her elation gone. She knew how fond Kevin was of his mother. She had brought up nine children without complaining. Sadie felt ashamed of her outburst earlier.

'I'd better tell you the other bad news,' he said. 'I'll be out of a job on Friday, though the woman at the bureau thinks there's a good chance of another. Digging roads again!' He spoke bitterly. She looked at him with surprise: it was unlike him to speak with bitterness.

'Me ma always said bad luck always comes in threes,' said Sadie. 'We've had our three now: getting burgled, your mother, and now your job.'

'That's a load of rubbish, old wives' tales. I've no time for them.'

'O.K. Keep your hair on.'

They did not talk much over their meal. Afterwards Sadie washed the dishes and Kevin dried them and then they sat down again in front of the fire, the only place in the room where it was warm. The same old thing every evening, thought Sadie, immediately banning the thought from her mind like an evil suggestion. They could hear the television blaring in the room next door. If the sound had been a little higher they could have heard the actual words. As it was it was just enough to annoy them.

'Wish we'd a telly,' said Sadie.

'Wish we'd a lot of things.'

'We can't sit here like this every night. I'll do my nut.'

'Want to go for a walk?'

'Not really.'

They sat, half-mesmerized by the noise of the television. It sounded like a Western film, judging from the music and the thud of horses' hooves. Kevin, tired after the hard day's work out of doors and the long walk home, lay back with his eyes half-closed, thinking he should write to his father. He hated writing letters. His lids sank down, flickered up for a brief moment before resting on his eyes again. Sadie muttered, shook her head. She would have to take up knitting, there was nothing else for it. She hated knitting, always had from the time her mother had tried to teach her when she was six years old. 'You're all thumbs, Sadie! For dear sake, will you pay attention?' She missed her mother and she had never thought she would. Her mother had a tongue as tart as a lemon and she was narrow and bigoted in what she believed and yet . . .

Sadie kicked Kevin in the shin. His eyes jerked open in panic. 'Wake up,' she said. 'It's like living with an ould man sitting here every night watching you sleeping.'

He sat up, yawning and rubbed his eyes. 'I believe I was clean away there.'

'Kevin, what are we going to do?' she demanded.

'How do you mean?'

'Well, we can't go on like this, can we?'

'I don't know. Maybe we can't do anything else?'

'We could go back to Belfast.'

'Go back to Belfast?' he said slowly. 'But, Sadie, think of all the trouble –'

'Ach, we can take the lot on,' she said scornfully. 'I don't care about a few bombs. There are parts of the town we can live where there's no trouble and nobody'd know us, but we could go and see our families. Anyway, I hate this place. I want to go back to Belfast.'

'Yes, I suppose so do I.'

Turning to look at one another, the decision formed gradually but surely between them.

'Shall we go then?' asked Kevin.

Sadie nodded. 'Let's.'

They no longer hunched over the fire. Kevin, in a mood of cheerfulness, set to work on a radio he had bought for a few pence, whistling as he sorted out the bits and pieces. To get away from this room and the drudge of trying to live and breathe in London! Sadie sang as she packed their suitcases. They could not go for a week but she wanted to pack now so that she could really believe they were going.

'I shall give notice to Mrs Kyrakis tomorrow,' she said gaily. 'In writing. And I shall tell ould Cullen, that boot-faced female at work, that she can stuff her stupid job from Saturday on!'

They would collect their pay at the end of the week, clear up the room on Sunday and cross on the overnight ferry on Monday. Kevin would easily get a job somewhere in Ulster, he might get a job on a farm and then they could live in the country. They loved the country though they forgot that evening that they liked the city too, and that they were essentially city dwellers who were miserable if they were deprived for long of streets to walk. Tonight they were optimistic and buoyant: they were leaving London and going home.

Kevin screwed the back on to the radio. He turned the knob and music poured into the room.

'It works!' he cried.

'Hurrah!' shouted Sadie. 'It's a good omen. Things are changing for us. For the better!'

They went to bed that night feeling happier than they had done for days.

Chapter Six

Five to seven on a grey winter's morning. This was one when Sadie did not mind putting her bare feet on the icy linoleum and standing in front of the fire to dress, with the calves of her legs scorching and the rest of her body tingling with cold. She sang. They were going home. Home! She would go into the kitchen and there would be her mother in her rollers and overall flipping over the bacon in the pan and her father would be sitting in his chair reading the paper and then Tommy would come in from the shipyard in his overalls . . .

'The kettle's boiling,' said Kevin.

The room was full of steam. Sadie seized the kettle, made the tea. Kevin tried the wireless: it still worked.

'Boys, am I not the clever one!' he said with a grin. 'We'll be able to get the seven o'clock news.'

The first item on the news was about Ulster. Two soldiers had been shot in Belfast during the night, one was dead, the other seriously ill. A bomb had exploded in a public house: two people were injured, the rest escaped with minor cuts and bruises. And a young girl had been tarred and feathered for going out with British soldiers.

'A normal night in Belfast from the sounds of it,' said Kevin with the same bitterness in his voice again. Sadie glanced at him uneasily as she poured the tea. Crouching in front of the electric fire she made the toast and listened to the news reader giving fuller details of the incidents.

Sadie knew the pub. Sometimes Tommy went there for a pint. But she couldn't believe that Tommy would have been there. She didn't want to believe it. Anyway, she told herself, no one had been killed. And then she saw how terrible it was when you had to be grateful if someone was *only* injured and had escaped with his life.

'Sadie!' said Kevin, touching her arm. 'Listen!'

Her mind had wandered away from the broadcast and was thinking of Tommy.

'It's Kate Kelly,' said Kevin. Sadie frowned, and he added, 'The girl that's been tarred and feathered.'

They listened. The girl's name was repeated again as Kate Kelly and the area of the city in which she lived was named too. It was Kevin's district.

'It must be the same one,' whispered Sadie.

A crowd of women had taken the girl, tied her to a lamp-post, and cut her hair off, and then she had been tarred and feathered. She had been associating with a member of the British army, a woman had told the reporter. Another girl, a friend of Kate's, had tried to help her but the women had held her back. No one else had gone to her aid. The girl who had been tarred and feathered was now in hospital suffering from shock.

'The Transport and General Workers' Union ...'

Kevin switched off the radio abruptly, and the room seemed very quiet. Kevin had worked for Kate Kelly's father who owned a junkyard near Kevin's house. Kate had been sweet on Kevin for a long time, he had taken her out once or twice but that was all, and when he had left Belfast he had not felt very kindly towards her for she had involved him in some trouble with the police. But he had forgiven her that and could not stomach the idea of her being shorn and tarred whilst she was tied helpless to a lamp-post.

'I don't understand,' said Sadie. 'Would she go out with a soldier? I thought she was hanging around with some IRA Provisional?'

'Ach, Kate doesn't think what she's about. She's got about

as much wit as a sparrow. But she doesn't deserve to be treated like that,' said Kevin. 'She's not one who cares about politics or issues. She probably saw a soldier and fancied him and never stopped to think she'd be accused of fraternising with the enemy! Bit of an eejit, there's no getting away from it.'

'It's horrible,' cried Sadie. 'Horrible! Just think, it could have been Brede.'

'No,' said Kevin. 'Brede's too careful. She's a peacemaker. But I'm thinking it could have been Brede who tried to help her. She wouldn't stand at the back and not help a friend in trouble.' Kevin's face darkened. 'If those women have harmed Brede I'll kill them!'

'It wouldn't help anything,' said Sadie quietly. Often she had said such things and then Kevin had quietened her. She put her hand on his shoulder. It was good to have someone to sort things out with: it helped you to get your balance.

'Give us another cup of tea, Sadie love.' Kevin held out the cup.

'Have you time?'

'I'm making it this morning.' He held the cup steady whilst she poured the tea.

'We always seem to be drinking tea,' said Sadie. 'Like me ma and her cronies. I never thought I'd be doing it.'

'It helps keep us warm. Sadie, I don't know what gets into people that they have to be as vicious as that.'

'Poor Kate,' said Sadie, taking Kevin's hand.

Kate had not liked Sadie, of course, for she was a Protestant and had attracted Kevin from the first time they met, but all of that did not matter now. Sadie could feel what it would be like to be tied to a lamp-post, cords binding your arms, women jeering around you, their faces full of venom, and then the tar thick and sticky covering your scalp, trickling down into your eyes and threatening to blind you . . . She shivered.

'How could we live there, Kevin?' she said softly. 'How could we? You and I together.'

He squeezed her hand. 'No, you're right, we couldn't. Maybe we'll be able to go back home some day when it's all settled . . .'

How it would be settled they could not begin to imagine. Kevin got up, lifted his jacket.

'Your lunch!' cried Sadie. 'I've nothing ready.'

'Never mind. I'll buy a pie or something like that.'

'Promise?'

'Promise.'

He kissed her and went, walking quickly today for he was late, but still stopping for a brief moment at the other side of the window as he always did. Sadie took the suitcases from under the bed and unpacked them.

At lunch-time she bought two orange mugs and a remnant of orange material which would be about the right size to cover the old brown velveteen cushion in the armchair. The purchases cheered her, and when she returned to the cloakroom she opened the parcel and showed them to Rita.

'Nice colours,' said Rita. 'Do you like being married?'

'Oh yes.'

'Wouldn't change places with you myself. Won't catch me getting married for a few years yet. I want a good time first.'

'But I do have a good time,' said Sadie. 'With Kevin.'

She hurried home after work that day, running to catch trains, pushing and shoving with the rest to make sure she would not be left behind.

The light was on: Kevin was home.

'I've got a surprise for you,' he said, holding his hands behind his back. 'Shut your eyes.'

She shut her eyes, opened them when he told her to. He was holding two yellow mugs. She laughed.

'Don't you like them?'

'Sure they're the loveliest mugs I ever set eyes on.' She pulled the paper off her parcel. 'And what about these?'

'Well,' said Kevin eyeing the two orange mugs she held

out, 'I would say they're the loveliest mugs I ever set eyes on.'

'Now we can have visitors,' said Sadie.

'That's right,' said Kevin. 'We shall have to consider carefully who we'll ask.'

'The Queen and the Duke of Edinburgh?'

Kevin made a face. 'Let's have somebody groovey!'

After tea Sadie sewed the cushion cover and Kevin wrote a letter to his father and a separate one to his mother. The radio played, the mugs shone on the shelf, and the piece of orange material glowed between Sadie's hands.

'I think we'll save for a lamp,' she said. 'And then we won't need to have that horrible light on over our heads. It'll be cosier that way.'

It was the best evening that they had had for a while.

Sadie loved Wednesdays. To finish work at one o'clock seemed to her ideal. On her way home she bought some little cakes and Demerara sugar. She cleaned the room, set out the mugs and plumped up the orange cushion. She looked round. The place did not look too bad after all.

Lara came promptly at three carrying the baby and a bunch of bronze chrysanthemums. She offered the flowers shyly to Sadie.

'They're lovely!' Sadie buried her face in the fresh moist flowers. 'Thank you very much, Lara. I love flowers.'

'That's good,' said Lara with a smile. The baby gurgled.

'Please come in,' said Sadie. 'You are my very first visitors!'

Lara said that she was honoured. She settled herself in the armchair with her back against the orange cushion. Sadie made coffee and gave the baby a drink of orange juice. He crawled around the floor investigating all the things in the room, quickly getting grubby. Lara said she did not mind, a little dirt did not harm him. She sat back looking serene and composed. In the evening Sadie told Kevin that she intended to be like that some day, unruffled and serene, taking everything in her stride without ever blowing a fuse. When she was eighty she might be, Kevin said.

Sadie chattered, telling Lara about Ulster and their families and how they would like to go home but couldn't.

'Yes,' said Lara. 'It is difficult to make a mixed marriage. I myself would not do it.'

'You wouldn't?'

Lara shook her head. 'There is less chance of success. I have seen many marriages of my friends to white men. They have lots of troubles and so do their children. I think it is better when like sticks to like.'

'Oh,' said Sadie, nonplussed.

'That doesn't mean I disapprove of you marrying a man of a different religion. Everyone must make up her own mind.'

'Kevin and I have no troubles between us. It's only other people that cause it.'

'You will have some difficulty. When you have children.' Lara smiled. 'But I am sure you will manage.'

Children, thought Sadie, who had not thought about them before except in the vague sense of realizing that she would probably have some one day.

'Kevin will want them brought up Catholic,' she said slowly.

'And you?'

'I don't fancy them going to confession and crossing themselves . . .' Sadie stopped. 'Ach well, it's a while off yet. I'll not worry about that.'

She told Kevin of their conversation in the evening. He was bent over the radio fiddling with some wires at the back and did not look up.

'I suppose they'll need to be brought up as Catholics, won't they?' said Sadie. 'Your church'll make you.'

Kevin shrugged. 'It's not exactly a case of making you.'

'Oh well!' Sadie sat down beside him on the floor and

hugged her knees with her arms. 'I suppose I'll get used to the idea.'

'Matter of fact there was something I was wanting to ask you.' Kevin still kept his head bent over the radio, 'Do you remember, I mentioned it the other day?'

Sadie frowned. 'Why don't you look at me?'

He lifted his head. 'Well, it's about getting married,' he spoke hesitantly.

'But we are married,' said Sadie. 'We got married at Gretna Green. We've got a certificate to prove it.'

'Aye, I know that. But the church doesn't. As far as it's concerned we're not.'

'I don't care what it thinks,' cried Sadie.

'But I do,' said Kevin.

'Do you mean –?' She was speechless.

'Yes, I do,' he said. 'Sadie, I want you to marry me in a Catholic church.'

Chapter Seven

Sadie exploded. Kevin had expected her to. He sat with his back against the wall working with the radio and allowed her to deliver her tirade. She had never set foot in a Catholic church in her life and she never would, it made her feel funny just to think about it. Her da had always told her the Church of Rome was evil and you had to be constantly on your guard against it or it would suck you in and you'd never get free of it. 'My da'd have a blue fit,' she said. 'He's an Orangeman. Have you forgotten that?'

'How could I forget a thing like that? But he doesn't come into it. And you've never paid heed to a thing he's said to you so why should you now? He's miles away.'

'Maybe he'd more sense than I thought.'

'For dear sake, what are you afraid of? Nobody'll bite you or even try to convert you.'

'Will they not?' she said darkly. 'Those priests try to get their hands on everybody.'

'Away ye go! You're as ignorant as the day I met you. I thought you'd got rid of all your old prejudices.'

'Prejudices!' She was spluttering. 'What about yourself? You're prejudiced against the Orange Order.'

'What Catholic wouldn't be? It's anti-Catholic. But you're no Orangewoman, Sadie.' He grinned. 'If you were you wouldn't be here with me now.'

'How do you know what I am?' she demanded.

'Do you know yourself?'

'Course I do!'

'Well then?'

'I'm a Protestant, aren't I?'

'That doesn't mean you're for the Orange Order. Oh, I know you used to swing your wee baton for the Orange parades and all that, but you saw the light and gave it up years back.' He grinned. 'When you met me.'

'So you're the brave boy that knows what's right and wrong! I suppose you're right pleased with yourself, thinking you made a convert. Well, I'm not sure, Kevin McCoy, that I might not be going back to thinking the Orangemen are right after all. The Order was founded to protect us from you lot! You attacked us first.' The thought of it fired her. She remembered sitting on her father's knee as a child, and him telling her stories of Catholics firing houses of Protestants, plundering and murdering, refusing to live at peace. She faced Kevin with anger, as if he were personally responsible.

'That's all history. Couple of hundred years back, for dear sake!' Kevin put down the screw-driver and held out his hands to her. 'Listen, Sadie, I'm not asking you to become Catholic. I'm only asking you to marry me in church because it'd make me happier. Then I'd feel truly married to you for ever and ever.'

'But I feel married to you for ever and ever without going through all that.' She stood up. 'Kevin, I couldn't stand the smell of incense and all those statues ... I'm sorry, I just couldn't. It gives me the shivers.'

'But you've never been in a Catholic church so you don't know how the incense smells or what the statues are like or anything! All you know is what you've been told by a lot of bigoted eejits!'

'So my parents are bigoted eejits now, are they?'

'You've said so yourself many a time.'

'I can say what I like about them but you can't.' Her eyes were full of fire, sparkling in the light. His were dark, like deep unfriendly pools. 'It's a horrible religion. It tries to own people body and soul. It gives me the dry boke!'

'What did you marry me for then?' he demanded. 'Am I not one of them?'

'My head must have been cut!'

'If that's the way you see it then there's no point in talking further.' He seized his jacket and was gone out of the house slamming the door.

She stood in the centre of the room fuming with rage. Her da had been right when he said never trust a Mick. She put on her coat and went out, determined to walk the streets till she was exhausted and Kevin would come back and wonder what had happened to her and when she didn't return he would start to worry. He might imagine she had run away for good or had been knocked down or had jumped over a bridge in her agony. She walked fast, her rage boiling inside her like a pot with a hot fire under it. She walked so fast and was so immersed in her rage that she did not notice where she was going. Her feet moved in long fast strides eating up the pavements.

Someone whistled behind her. It did not penetrate her mind at first. When it came the second time she looked round in irritation and saw a young man in a leather jacket approaching her.

'Hi,' he said. She walked on, he caught her arm.

'Leave go,' she said, trying to shake him off. 'Stupid devil!'

He laughed, and it was then that she noticed that she had wandered far from their district. She did not know this place at all, even though she and Kevin had walked so much. Perhaps it was the dark that changed it. The street was badly lit, full of dense shadows. The houses were poor, more run down even than the one they lived in. There were only a few houses in the street; the rest of it was covered by a large brick warehouse. And no one else was about. An eerie quiet seemed to hang between the rooftops. For a moment Sadie felt fear and then a wave of anger washed it away.

She lifted her foot and kicked him as hard as she could on

the shin. He yelped, his grip slackened momentarily, and she was away. She had a few yards start on him. He came after her but she was swift on her feet and at school no one had been able to beat her when it came to running. She outstripped him easily and only stopped once she was in the main road. When she came to the first Underground station she took the first tube home. On the train she thought again of Kevin. Because of him she had been attacked. Well . . . almost attacked. In her head she held a conversation in which she told Kevin how she had been near done to death and how sorry he would be and beg her forgiveness. So absorbed was she that she nearly missed her stop again and had to jump off quickly. Trains had a habit of doing that to her. Her mind travelled far and wide on her journeys on the Underground.

On the way up the street she rehearsed what she would say. Perhaps it would be better to be cool and give out an air of quiet suffering with fortitude. That would make him feel worse.

The curtains of their room were drawn but chinks of light showed round the edges. She passed the West African in the hall who eyed her with interest. She smiled back at him too though not too encouragingly. She flung open the door, word forming on her lips. Kevin was not there. And there was no sign that he had been back at all.

Kevin walked to the nearest pub when he left Sadie. He was not much of a drinking man but pubs were somewhere warm to go where you could meet other people and pass the time of day with a chat or a game of darts.

Sadie was an idiot, he told himself as he paid for a half pint of beer and lifted the foaming glass to his mouth; she had a passion for exaggeration and a devil inside her that made her push things to extremes. He would let her cool off for a while and then go back and they would make it up.

He stood with his back to the bar looking round. Some men were playing darts, others were sitting over a game of dominoes. Two girls of around his own age sat together. They were watching him; he looked away. One of the girls got up and came over to the bar.

'Two shandies,' she said to the barman. She rested her elbow on the counter and glanced at Kevin. She tilted her chin. 'Stranger round here, are you?'

'I'm living near by.'

'Oh you are! Never seen you before. You're Irish, aren't you?'

'Yes.'

'Thought so. You can tell. You're a good-looking feller.'

He stared at her unblinkingly. She was what his mother would call a brazen hussey. He wanted to laugh. His mouth twitched at the corners; she mistook it for a smile and gave him one back.

'Going to join us?' she asked, nodding over at the other girl.

'No, sorry. You see,' he said, lowering his voice as if it was an important secret, 'I'm a married man.'

He moved off down the pub. A married man indeed! He scarcely felt it. It was a hard thing to feel. Not that he wanted to be going out with any other girl. He would not do that to Sadie. He stopped by the men playing darts and watched them.

After a few minutes one of the men turned to him and said, 'Want a game?'

'Sure.'

Kevin proved to have a steady hand and a good aim. He scored better than anyone else. They'd need to get him in their darts team, they said.

'What do you say?' said the man who had first invited him to play.

'O.K. with me,' said Kevin.

He sat down with the man whose name was Bob Green.

'Call me Bob,' he said. 'Everyone does. Never mind my grey hairs. Now, come on and tell me a thing or two about yourself.'

Kevin did, and Bob listened with interest. 'So you're wanting a new job,' he said. 'I must know somebody who could help you. I know most people round here. I've lived in this part of London all my life. What kind of thing are you after?'

'Don't really know. I'd like to do something with my hands. I like working with radios. Things like that.'

'With radios . . . I know someone with a radio and television shop. Tell you what, I'll have a word with him. O.K?'

'That'd be great,' said Kevin.

'Can't promise anything of course but I'll do my best.'

They arranged to meet the following evening. Kevin walked home whistling.

'Hey, Sadie,' he called as he opened the door. 'I met a man in the pub who might be able to get me a job.'

Sadie, who was sitting hunched over the fire, looked up and scowled at him.

'What's up with you?' he asked. 'You've got a face as long as a fiddle on you.'

'No wonder!' she cried. 'Seems you've forgot. I got lost and was attacked by a horrible man –'

'Did he hurt you?'

'No. But it was no thanks to you that he didn't.'

'You're good at taking care of yourself.' He sat down and took off his boots.

'Kevin McCoy, you don't seem a bit bothered that your wife was attacked. There was I fighting for my life and you were getting drunk.'

'I had one half pint and played a game of darts. I won too. They're going to put me on the team.'

'Bully for you! You look right pleased with yourself.'

'But I've got a lead for a job, Sadie! Aren't you pleased?'

'Of course,' she said gruffly. All the boiling rage had long since subsided and left her with a simmering resentment. She had sat too long waiting for him to come back and could not even remember half of the things she had intended to say.

Besides, she was too relieved to see him. He might be an eejit and a lot of other things besides but he was still her Kevin and when he came to her and put his arms round her she pressed her face against his and hugged him tight and happiness flooded back into her pushing out all the bad feelings. When they were getting ready for bed she said, 'About that getting married business . . .'

'Oh yes?' He got into bed.

'I'll have to think it over carefully. I'll let you know in a few days.'

'Fine,' he said, and when she turned round she saw that he was asleep.

'Honest!' she said, shaking her head. 'Men!'

She lay in bed watching the reflection of the street light on the ceiling. Sometimes a car passed in the street and its headlights fanned across their room cutting easily through the flimsy curtains. Someone was having a party across the street: she could hear the music and laughter. Overhead feet moved incessantly. Somewhere else in the house a record player was going. Feet passed the window. There seemed to be noise and movement in the street for most of the night. She did not mind for she liked the feel of people round her, liked the idea of them eating and sleeping and dancing and talking, all so different, but all alive and struggling to make the best of things. She thought of Lara and her baby and that made her feel warm. It was nice to have a friend.

Beside her Kevin breathed deeply and steadily. She wished he didn't want her to have a church ceremony. He was right: she was a bit afraid of going into a Catholic church. Of course she didn't really expect priests to get hold of her but something inside her rose up at the idea of walking into a Catholic church and standing in front of the altar and letting a priest marry her.

Chapter Eight

Bob Green brought his friend Mr Davis to the pub the following evening. Kevin had been watching the door for an hour before they arrived.

'Well, lad,' said Mr Davis, settling himself down on the bench beside Kevin after they had been introduced. 'I hear you're after a job. Bob's told you I have a radio and television business?'

'Yes, yes he has.'

'What experience have you?'

'None. But I've done a lot of messing around with radios on my own.'

'Hum,' said Mr Davis and lifted his frothing glass to his lips.

Kevin sat back, hope fading in him. There was little chance that he would get such a job. It would be the same old story all over again. Sorry, you're unqualified, inexperienced. Go back to your unskilled labouring and dig roads and flatten sites so that men can build on them.

'What are you sighing about?' demanded Mr Davis, looking over the top of his glass at Kevin. He was a red-faced man with bulging eyes. They bulged now at Kevin, rather ferociously.

'I'm thinking I've little chance. Nobody'll let you even try.'

'Well, I'm not keen on taking on greenhorns. But I was one myself once. I might be prepared to give you a chance if you'd go to evening classes.'

'Indeed I would,' said Kevin. 'Sure the chance is all I'm asking for.'

'I like the look of you, lad. I don't think you would let me down.'

'I wouldn't, Mr Davis, honest.'

'You'd have a lot to learn, but if you're willing that's the main thing.'

'I am willing, Mr Davis. Very willing.' Kevin kept his eyes fixed on the man's face.

'Shall we say, start on Monday then?'

'Monday,' said Kevin, his throat dry. He had a job! And not a labouring one at that. Wait till he got home and told Sadie!

Mr Davis took Kevin to his shop. It was only a short walk away. In the back room radios and televisions stood around with their backs stripped off, wires hanging out. Mr Davis said that it was not such a mess as it looked, he knew what he was doing. Kevin nodded, listening carefully to everything the older man said.

'I've worked with radios all my life,' said Mr Davis. 'Well, lad, see you Monday morning then?

Kevin bought fish and chips and Coca-Cola on the way home. He found Sadie squatting on the floor cutting out another cushion cover.

'What a gorgeous smell!'

'Fish and chips.' He swung the bag on to the table. 'We're going to have ourselves a wee bit of a celebration, Sadie my love.'

She leapt to her feet. 'You got a job?'

' 'Deed I did get a job. And I think I'm going to like it fine.' He opened the Coca-Cola and poured it into the yellow mugs. 'Funny looking colour in there,' he said, making a face at it, 'but never mind.'

Sadie raised her mug. 'Here's to the new job.' They drank and then she asked him what wage he was getting. When he told her she frowned. 'But that's only half what you're getting now,' she said.

He shrugged. 'I know, but I'm only starting at this job. I have to go to night classes and get a qualification and then I'll get more money.'

'But how'll we manage in the meantime?' she wailed. 'It's been hard enough as it is, what with this rent and all.'

'Labouring's well paid, Sadie, but it's a terrible job and I'm not wanting to do it for ever.'

She had had plans for new curtains. She had seen material in the store that day and had measured up the window when Kevin was out. His face, which had been beaming when he came in, was now sobered.

'We'll manage,' she said, opening the parcel of fish and chips. The aroma rose up making the saliva run in her mouth. 'We'll just have to wait a bit longer for that house in Kensington.'

Kevin's new job brought changes in their way of living. They could stay in bed for another half-hour in the morning. On those cold winter mornings it was bliss to lie under the warm blankets and listen to the feet passing on their way to work. Kevin now left at ten minutes to eight, just a few minutes before Sadie. He came home at lunch-time and was back before her in the evening.

'You might have made the bed,' she said one evening when she came back to find him sitting on it, unmade. He was reading a radio engineering book.

'I never thought,' he said, looking up from the book briefly and then back down at it again.

She made a face at the back of the book, set down her bag of groceries and took off her coat. She lit the gas ring, put on the frying pan and began to cook the meal.

'Will it be long?' he asked. 'I'll need to watch my time.'

'Oh, you'll be in time.'

'What's up with you? You sound fed up.'

'I am a bit. All this travelling on trains and working all day . . .'

'It's gone six,' he said, his eyes on the clock on the mantel-piece.

'O.K!'

She put out his meal, sat opposite him in silence whilst he ate. His eyes were far away. He was thinking about radio engineering. He seldom seemed to think of anything else these days. He went three evenings a week to classes, and on the others often played darts in the pub.

'Thanks, love,' he said, getting up quickly. 'I'll see you after. Oh, by the way, there's a letter from Brede on the mantelpiece. Our mother's doing rightly.'

After he had gone Sadie took Brede's letter from the mantel-piece and read it. Mrs McCoy had had a hysterectomy but the operation was successful. It was just as well she would have no more children, wrote Brede, for nine was enough for any woman. You're right, Brede, thought Sadie, except that nine was too many. Kevin had said he would not expect her to have a big family like that. The world couldn't take it any longer, as well as the women. Brede was still working as a nursery nurse. She was worried about the children, for even the little ones were being brain-washed into violence by the life around them. A day didn't pass without an explosion, a shooting, an injury or a death. 'You are lucky,' wrote Brede, 'to be away from it all.'

Brede's letter made Sadie feel homesick. She sat at the table and wrote to her brother Tommy. She wrote a funny letter that would make Tommy laugh. He'd shake his head and say, 'Sadie Jackson, you're a real terror yet!' She told him about Miss Cullen, and Mrs Kyrakis, and their fellow lodgers, making life in the shop and the house sound like a riot of fun and laughter. And she told him about Kevin's new job, but not that it took Kevin out so many nights a week. She finished the letter, put it in an envelope, addressed and stamped it. It lay on the table staring up at her. Mr Thomas Jackson. There was a lump in her throat. 'Silly ould fool that you are,' she said aloud to herself. She got up, put on her coat and went out to post it.

On the way back she called at Lara's. Krishna, Lara's husband opened the door. He stood with his hand on the edge of it, holding it firm, as if he was ready to close it against intruders.

'Yes?' he asked, his face expressionless.

'I was wondering if Lara was in,' faltered Sadie, thinking how stupid it sounded.

'Yes, she is in. She is busy with the baby.'

'I see.' Sadie backed away, stumbling over a piece of torn linoleum. 'It's all right, it wasn't important. I just wanted to ask her something. I'll see her tomorrow.'

Back in her room, Sadie saw that it was still only eight o'clock. It did not seem possible. She washed the few dirty plates, peeled the potatoes for the following night and listened to music on Radio One. She could not sit still. She went out into the passage of the house and listened, jumping guiltily when anyone opened a door. The woman with the felt slippers shuffled along the passage and Sadie delayed her for a few minutes in conversation. They talked about the woman's cats.

'I've three black and two white,' said the woman.

'Five cats?' Sadie's eyes were round.

She was taken into the woman's room to see them. The smell made Sadie blench as soon as the door was opened. The cats reclined arrogantly on cushions and chairs, yawning superciliously, stretching their paws. Saucers of half-eaten food lay around the floor.

'Nothing like cats,' said the woman. 'Better than people.'

Maybe she should get herself a cat, thought Sadie as she returned to their room. At least it would be something alive in the room beside herself, something to stroke and talk to. She suggested it to Kevin when he came in.

'A cat?' he said. 'Don't talk daft. We've enough on our

plates as it is.' His face was flushed with fresh air and excitement. 'The class is really great, Sadie.' He rubbed his hands together. 'Boys, I'm starving. Have you anything for us?'

'I'll see,' she said coolly, but he was too elated by his evening class to notice.

'Kevin, I'll go nuts if I sit in this room much more. London's a dead awful place.' She added vehemently, 'I can hardly wait to leave it.'

His face dropped. 'Sure I'm sorry to hear you say that. I'm just beginning to enjoy myself.'

Chapter Nine

Kevin had gone to the pub to play in a darts match and Sadie had just sat down to see if she could remember how to knit, when the priest called. She looked up, puzzled by the knock on the door, and put aside the knitting thankfully.

She opened the door. Never before had she stood face to face with one as she did now, looking into his eyes, and he looking back into hers as if butter wouldn't melt in his mouth!

'Does Kevin McCoy live here?' he asked, twirling his black hat round in his hand.

'He does,' she said. 'But he's not in.' She moved the door towards him but he had his foot well placed, just an inch of his toe over the threshold, but it was enough. Her ma had said often enough that priests tried to infiltrate themselves by all sorts of methods.

'Will he be back soon?' he asked.

'Not for hours. I could give him a message.'

'Oh, there's no message. I was just paying him a visit since he's in my parish. Perhaps I could come in and have a word with you myself? My name's Father Mulcahy. You must be Mrs McCoy?'

'Yes, but –'

And then he was in the room. She did not know afterwards if she opened the door or he pushed it, but the next thing she knew, there they were sitting at either side of the fire looking at one another.

'You're young to be married.' He smiled at her.

'I'm seventeen,' she said, not smiling back. She picked up her knitting and held it on her lap.

'That's young. You're just a child. What's your name? I can't call you Mrs McCoy.'

'Sadie.' She did not know why she told him. Inside her head she was holding another conversation entirely with him. It's none of your business what my name is and you can just go away right now for I'm not wanting to consort with a priest of Rome. Me da would take a fit if he could see me sitting here as meek as mild . . .

'How are you liking London?'

'I'm not.'

'Yes, it's a big place and takes a lot of getting used to. You won't know many people?' She shrugged and he added, 'if you were to come along to the church –'

'I'm a Protestant,' she said, lifting her chin defiantly and looking him straight in the eye for the first time.

'Oh, I see.'

'What's wrong with that?' she demanded.

'Nothing, nothing at all. Did I say that there was?'

'You looked at me very funny like.'

'That was just because I was surprised. Kevin hadn't told me he was married to a Protestant, that was all.' He leaned back against the chair as if he was settling in for the evening. He folded his hands in front of his stomach. 'But it's interesting, very interesting. It can't have been very easy for you in the North of Ireland.'

' 'Deed it wasn't. Neither my family nor Kevin's was for us at all.'

'Under the circumstances . . .' He spread out his hands. 'Who could blame them? Did they consent to your marriage?'

'We were married at Gretna,' she said.

'Ah!' Now he fitted his fingers together to make a steeple. 'So you married in a registry office? You realise then that in the eyes of the church you're not married at all?'

'Your church. Not mine.'

'But Kevin's.'

'Why are you always trying to get your hands on people?'

He laughed. 'You've got that wrong, you know, Sadie. Oh yes, we like to make converts, but what religion doesn't? If you believe in something strongly then you want to let others share it too.'

'Now look here,' said Sadie, warming to the argument, 'the church in Rome is after power . . .'

They talked all evening, or argued, as Sadie later described it to Kevin. In the midst of it she got up and made tea but did not stop talking. They were drinking tea when Kevin returned. He stood in the doorway astonished. Sadie's face was flushed and her eyes sparkled.

'Evening, Kevin,' said Father Mulcahy. 'Nice to see you, boy. I've been having a most enjoyable conversation with Sadie here. She's a great talker.'

'I know,' said Kevin, his eyes still on Sadie's face. 'But what have you been talking about?'

'The Roman church,' said Sadie. 'The supremacy of the pope. Things like that.'

'Well!' Kevin sat on a stool between them, rested his hands on his knees.

'It's done me good, Kevin, arguing with Sadie,' said Father Mulcahy. 'You need to sharpen your wits from time to time and question your beliefs.'

'I don't suppose you've budged an inch, have you?' said Sadie.

'No,' he said. 'Have you?'

'No.' She laughed.

Father Mulcahy stood up. 'I'll need to be getting along. I dropped in for ten minutes and stayed two hours. Hope I didn't keep you back, Sadie.'

'Sure I enjoyed the company,' she said.

Kevin looked at her wonderingly.

'By the way, Kevin,' said Father Mulcahy, 'we discussed the business of you getting married in church.'

'You did?'

'Sadie has agreed and we have fixed the date for a week on Saturday.'

'Sadie agreed?' Kevin stood up too.

'I decided I might as well be generous,' said Sadie loftily. 'After all, as Father Mulcahy pointed out to me, there's nothing for me to be afraid of so I can afford to be.'

Drizzling sleet was falling a week on Saturday. It disappeared as soon as it hit the grey pavement but it was cold when it slid down their necks and faces. They hurried through it with their collars pulled high.

'Happy's the bride the sun shines on,' said Sadie, as they reached the shelter of the church porch.

'We don't need sun.'

'Oh no?'

He took her hand and led her inside. The auditorium was chilly and deserted except for one woman who prayed in a pew with bowed head. Candles flickered in front of the altar. Sadie's eyes scanned the walls passing over statues of Jesus and the Virgin Mary and other saints unknown to her. There was a pervasive, slightly sweetish smell. She tried to suppress a giggle at the back of her throat but it came out causing a small ripple in the silence. Kevin's hand tightened over hers. She did not look up at him.

They came to the top of the aisle. Kevin paused in front of the high altar, genuflected and crossed himself. It made her feel uneasy watching him. She bent her head and wished she had never come. They *were* married after all.

Father Mulcahy came through a doorway to meet them, his black skirts swishing round his heels. A candle on the altar guttered and died.

The priest led them into a side chapel where two witnesses

waited, a man and a woman, whose names they never knew. Sadie and Kevin stood in front of Father Mulcahy. Sadie wiped the damp palms of her hands down the sides of her coat. It, too, was wet from the sleet. There's nothing to be afraid of she told herself, but she could not seem to stop the feeling inside her, of uneasiness and revulsion and expectation that something bad would come of all this. The priest had his eyes on her; he was speaking, he was marrying them, and she was not even listening. A jingle came into her head, one that they used to sing in the street.

> If I'd a penny,
> Do you know what I'd do?
> I'd buy a rope
> And hang the pope
> And let King Billy through.

She trembled, suppressing a giggle, and put her hand to her mouth. She coughed.

The priest was looking at her, asking her if she would have this man for her lawful wedded husband. She said that she would for that at least she was sure of. He was her husband already. She did not hear any of the other words. She made no promises about the church. She was vaguely aware that Kevin must be, he was muttering in her ear. And then he was slipping the ring back on to her finger. She had taken it off before they came out and gave it to him. 'What a carry on!' she had said, shaking her head.

Father Mulcahy was crossing himself now, as were Kevin and the two witnesses. Sadie stood straight, her eyes on the balding head of the priest.

'May I congratulate you?' said Father Mulcahy, offering them his hand. 'And wish you all the best in your life together.'

They followed him out of the chapel into a vestry to sign the register.

'Not so bad was it, Sadie?' he asked.

'No.' Kevin's hand found hers again. She had pleased him by going through with it; he let her know by the pressure of his fingers.

'She was feeling a bit strange, I think, Father,' said Kevin.

'I daresay. It takes a long time to get rid of fears you grow up up with. They go deep.'

'I wasn't afraid,' said Sadie indignantly.

'Good.' Father Mulcahy smiled and lifted the register. 'Now then, if you'll sign here . . .'

The sleet was still falling as they came out of the church. They stood in the porch watching it drive down on the street, closing it in, making the rest of the world seem remote.

'Grotty day.' Sadie shivered. 'Don't feel like going home all that much.'

'We're not going to,' said Kevin. 'I'm taking you out. We're going up to the West End. We're going to have a meal and go to the pictures.'

'Isn't that a grand idea?' she cried, her eyes lighting up.

'Sure, isn't it our wedding day, Mrs McCoy?' he said.

Chapter Ten

Their meal out cost so much that they had to live on tinned beans and bread and jam until pay day came round again.

'But it was worth it,' Sadie told Lara on Wednesday afternoon. Lara came in every Wednesday though she had never asked Sadie to her house in return. They were on their hands and knees on the floor cutting a skirt out of a remnant Sadie had bought in the shop. 'We hardly ever go out so it was a real treat. Do you go out often with your husband?' Sadie found it difficult to refer to him as Krishna since Lara did not do it herself.

Lara shook her head. 'No, very seldom.' She lifted the scissors. 'Shall I begin to cut?' she asked.

'Please.' Sadie caught hold of the baby who would have liked the flashing silver scissors for himself. Lara cut carefully. She seldom told Sadie anything of her life. She talked sometimes of her family in India but never of Krishna or her life with him. She came in every Wednesday for an hour or so and returned home well before Krishna would come along the street carrying his newspaper under his arm. Sadie smiled at him and said, 'Hello' and then he nodded, but nothing more.

'There,' said Lara, folding up the pieces. 'That didn't take long. You can sew it this evening.'

Sadie nodded. 'Kevin's got his evening class. I'm sick fed up with him going out so much.'

'You want him to advance in his career, don't you?'

'Oh yes of course.'

'Then you must make sacrifices too.'

'Trouble is I'm not very good at sacrifices.' Sadie made a rueful face at herself. 'I think you'd be better at that than me, Lara.' Lara smiled. 'I suppose you were brought up to be docile, you know, with men,' Sadie went on. 'I used to fight my brother, wouldn't let him tell me what to do.'

'It's not just a case of being docile,' said Lara. 'Sometimes it is not worth fighting. One has to save one's energy.'

'Well, I dunno. Maybe I'd be better if I'd been brought up with some of that wisdom of the East business too.'

Lara burst out laughing. 'Sadie, you are funny at times.'

'Glad I amuse you,' said Sadie good-naturedly. She filled the kettle to make coffee. 'I like having you coming in here every Wednesday, Lara. You're the only friend I've got.'

Lara hesitated. 'Sadie, I'm sorry I can't ask you to come and visit me. I hope you don't mind.'

'Course not,' said Sadie, though she did. She spooned coffee into the cups.

'It's Krishna –' Lara bit her lip.

'Doesn't he like me?'

'It's not that.'

'Is it because I'm white?'

'Oh no! It is just that he is very private. He does not like strangers.'

'But how can strangers ever become friends if you don't give them a chance in the first place?'

'I know.' Lara sighed. 'But you cannot force people. I am sorry.'

'That's all right. Don't worry about it.' Sadie gave Lara her coffee. 'You can always come here.'

Sadie noticed Lara taking a quick glance at her watch under her sari. Today they were later than usual having their coffee.

'Are you lonely in the evenings when your husband is out?' asked Lara. 'Why don't you go to an evening class yourself?'

'I might,' said Sadie without enthusiasm, 'if I'd someone to go with. What about you, Lara? Would you come with me? Hey, what about woodwork or something like that? Then we could show them. I've always liked banging in nails.'

'I'm afraid I could not. There is the baby.'

'Your husband could baby-sit.'

'I don't think so.' Lara put down her cup. 'I must go now, Sadie. See you next week.'

Next week was a long time. Seven days lay between. Weekends were good for then she and Kevin were together but the other evenings were stretches of time to be filled and she had never seen time in that way before.

'Lara's husband doesn't like strangers,' Sadie told Kevin at tea-time. 'And he's living surrounded by ten million. Not very friendly I call it.'

'Perhaps he's afraid,' suggested Kevin.

'Afraid? I never thought of that. In that case I'll go on smiling at him and saying good morning.' Sadie fiddled with the ends of her hair. 'I'll not be home at tea-time tomorrow, Kevin.'

That made him look up. 'Not be home?'

'I'm going out with the girls from work. You know they've been asking me for ages.'

'Oh.'

'I'll leave you something for your tea.'

He shrugged. 'I can get a pie in the pub.'

'You're annoyed, aren't you?' she said.

'I like seeing you when I get in.'

'But you only come in to go out again.'

'Now, Sadie, you know –'

'Oh yes, I know it all. But I'm not for sitting here night after night on my tod. You can't expect me to.'

He laid down his knife and fork. 'Where'll you go with the girls?'

She got up, lifted the plates, put her back to him. 'I don't know.' She ran water into the sink, squirted in a jet of washing-up liquid and splashed the plates noisily. He came up and stood behind her.

'You won't be going dancing or to a party or anything like that, will you?'

'What's it to you if I am?' She tilted her shoulder at him.

'You're my wife, that's what it is.'

'But you don't own me.' She turned to confront him.

'I wouldn't stand for you looking at another man,' he said. And he turned and went out.

She was excited. It was a long time since she had got herself ready to go out for an evening with a crowd of girls. There were six of them in the cloakroom giggling and laughing, doing their hair, making up their faces. She slipped her dress over her head. It was black. She had not had a black dress before but Rita had said it would go nicely with her hair. She had bought it in the store on credit.

'Will I do you up, love?' asked Rita.

'Thanks.' Sadie turned her back to let Rita pull up the zip.

'Hey,' said Rita, 'you look real cool. You'll knock them all cold.'

'Don't be daft,' said Sadie, and for the first time felt a little uneasy about the outing. She didn't want to knock anybody cold, except Kevin.

She put on eyeshadow and mascara lent by Rita. She did not often bother for she was usually in a hurry and Kevin liked her better without. It made her look older, more sophisticated. She twisted her head one way and then the other, looking at her face in the mirror. Then she laughed. If she didn't watch she'd end up a right eejit!

'What's the joke?' asked Rita. She was puffing clouds of lacquer on to her hair. Sadie ducked out of the stream.

'I was just thinking about me, an old married woman, going out for a night on the town.'

'Well, why not?' said Rita. 'That man of yours leaves you

alone often enough. You're too young yet for the grave.' She tucked her arm through Sadie's and said, 'Come on then, duck!'

They went to a Chinese restaurant for a meal. Rita advised Sadie on what to eat and Sadie discovered that she rather liked the food. The girls talked at the top of their voices, told jokes that were not very funny and laughed a great deal. They were all friendly to Sadie now: she had been accepted.

From there they went to a discotheque. As she gave up her coat and followed Rita into the dim, hot, noisy room, Sadie thought of Kevin sitting at a desk listening to the teacher. She tripped over a step.

'Watch it!' said Rita. 'You're not drunk yet.'

'I've no intention of getting drunk,' said Sadie. 'That's a mug's game.'

But Rita wasn't listening. No one could in this noise. Drums banged, guitars zinged, someone was singing. Lights began to revolve around the room.

Rita was tugging at her arm. 'Don't just stand there,' she shouted in her ear. 'Come on and meet the crowd.'

The crowd was a bunch of young men. Someone bought her a drink which she couldn't identify in the twilight but it tasted strong and almost choked her going over her throat. She poured it into an empty glass when no one was looking.

She sat down, for her feet were tired after a day of standing behind the counter but she was not allowed to sit. She was hauled up by a young man in black with long fair hair. That was all she could make out about him. He pulled her on to the floor to dance. They were all dancing, writhing and twisting, close together. Against her inclination the music caught her, and she began to move, forgetting the others and the boy in black who circled round her like a large shadow.

In a lull in the music he said, 'I'm Joe. Who are you?'

'Sadie,' she said, and then the music swelled up again.

She danced all evening. Her body felt alive, full of energy, possessed by the music. Rita was right: she was too young to sit in a room and knit and wait for a man to come home and talk about radio engineering.

'We're all going back to my place,' said Rita.

'O.K.,' said Sadie, ready now to be one of them.

Rita shared a tiny flat with two other girls. Her room was crammed with furniture and every piece of furniture was covered with clothes, magazines, packets of cigarettes, unwashed dishes. They packed into the room like sardines, pushing aside the clothes and dirty cups. The boys passed round beer and everyone drank from the can.

Sadie found herself sitting on the floor beside Joe. Now that there was more light she saw that he was about twenty or so, with a fringe of reddish beard round his chin, and dark blue eyes. If she had not been married she would have thought him attractive. He put his hand over hers where it lay on the floor. She slid hers out.

'What's up?' he asked.

'I'm married,' she said solemnly.

'I don't mind,' he said and took her hand again.

'But I do.' She removed her hand.

'What did you want to get married for?'

'Why do people usually get married?'

'Search me.' He raised his beer can to his lips.

She decided that she did not like him after all, which was fortunate. Kevin was worth ten of him. Kevin . . . She looked at her watch and jumped up.

'I must go, Rita. I'll miss my train.'

'One of the boys'll run you home. Harry's got a van and –' Rita grinned '– Joe there has a motor bike. I'm sure he'd like to take you home.'

'I'll just get the train,' said Sadie hurriedly.

She pulled on her coat. Joe leant back against the wall and watched her idly, rather like a spider watching a fly. But she was not in his web.

'It's been great, Rita. See you tomorrow.'

She ran all the way to the station and caught the last train home.

Kevin was in bed, the light turned off, pretending to sleep.

'Sorry I'm so late,' she said. 'But we went back to Rita's place afterwards and I missed a train . . . Oh all right, you can kid on you're sleeping if you want. See if I care!'

In the morning they were cool and polite to one another. He passed the margarine as if he had never seen her before. And he went out without kissing her good-bye. It was the first time he had ever done it.

'Joe's gone overboard for you,' said Rita, when Sadie arrived in the cloakroom. 'He was asking all about you when you'd gone.'

'I hope you told him I wasn't the type to play around.'

'It's up to you to tell him what you like,' said Rita.

'I won't be seeing him,' said Sadie.

'Like to bet?'

Joe came in to the store just after Miss Marshall had gone to lunch. Rita must have told him, Sadie thought, as she looked up and saw him crossing the floor.

'I'll have a card of elastic,' he said, leaning on the counter.

She took out a card and laid it beside him. 'That'll be five pence,' she said.

He looked at the elastic. 'I'd rather have pink.'

She raked in the box, replaced it with pink. 'Five pence,' she said.

He fished five pence from his pocket. 'You can keep the change.'

'Thanks a lot.' She rang it up in the till.

Miss Cullen passed. She frowned when she saw Joe leaning against the counter. She looked back over her shoulder and he looked back at her.

'That your boss?'

'Yes.'

'When are you coming out with me?'

'I'm not.'

'Why not?'

'I told you –'

'O.K. so you're married. I told you I didn't mind.'

'And I told you I did.'

'That's your problem then, isn't it?'

She went up to the other end of the counter, he followed her. Miss Cullen came back through the store again. She stopped.

'Everything all right, Sadie?' She looked at Joe.

'Fine,' said Sadie.

'I'm buying elastic,' said Joe, waving the card in the air.

'Sadie, you might at least have wrapped it for the gentleman,' said Miss Cullen reprovingly.

'I'd like it wrapped up,' said Joe.

Sadie wrapped the card, Miss Cullen moved on.

'Slipping, aren't you?' said Joe.

'Why don't you take yourself off?'

'Your husband's probably out with some bird at night when he says he's at the evening class.'

'He's not like that,' said Sadie.

'No?' Joe laughed.

'Not all men are like you.'

He leant on the counter until Miss Marshall returned from lunch.

'You off duty now then?' he said, as Sadie lifted her bag and came round to the front of the counter. 'I'll buy you lunch.'

'Thanks, but I'd rather starve.'

She walked up the stairs to the cloakroom where she ate her sandwiches and remained for the rest of her break.

At half-past five when she came out of the shop, he was there, leaning against the wall. He tagged along beside her and Rita.

'Told you he was keen, didn't I?' said Rita.

'And persistent,' he added.

'You can persist all you like,' said Sadie. 'It won't do you any good.'

'We'll see,' he said.

He followed her to the station, got on the same train, changed stations with her and got on the train that would take her to her home station.

'You're a real nut,' she said as they stood side by side, hanging on to the overhead straps.

'I like being a nut. It amuses me.'

They left the train, travelled by escalator up to the street.

'I live along there,' she said, 'and my husband will be waiting for me.'

'That's all right by me.'

'He's six foot one in his stocking soles and he's Irish. He has a terrible temper when he's roused.' She thought she saw Joe's feet move less eagerly. She added, 'He'd make mince meat of you, I'm giving you fair warning.'

'If you promise to have lunch with me I'll leave you now,' said Joe.

She walked on. 'You're not blackmailing me.'

He caught her up, fell into step. They rounded the corner and walked straight into Kevin.

Chapter Eleven

'Men are stupid,' said Sadie.

'Some of them,' said Rita, who was back-combing her hair in front of the mirror. Sadie sat on her unmade bed, watching her. 'Who're you thinking of? Joe?'

'And Kevin. Both of them!'

Rita turned round. 'What's Kevin been doing to you then?'

Sadie told her how Joe had followed her home and they had met Kevin. 'Kevin took the huff at me. He wouldn't believe Joe had just followed me. He said boys don't follow girls unless they think they're on to something.'

'He doesn't know Joe. He's a right nut that boy. But he really fancies you, you know, Sadie.'

'That's what Kevin thought. We had a row and I burnt the sausages as black as cinders and the place was full of smoke and then he went off to his evening class and left me –' Sadie paused for breath. 'So I thought I'd come on over and see you.'

'Glad you did.'

Sadie enjoyed the evening. It was cosy, sitting by the fire chatting to Rita, drinking cups of coffee, and not having to worry about anything. They talked mostly about boys and Rita said that she didn't see why Sadie shouldn't go out with Joe. 'You might get to like him,' she said, looking slyly at Sadie.

'But, Rita, I'm married!'

'Oh that! It'll never last.'

The words made Sadie feel cold inside; the evening was no longer cosy, and she wanted to go home. Rita went on smoking and talking about Joe. He was a restless boy, in and out of work. At the moment he was not working: that was why he could hang around the shop half the day.

'I must go,' said Sadie, getting up abruptly.

She met Kevin coming up the street on her way home.

'Where've you been?' he asked.

'Rita's.'

'You saw that fellow Joe, didn't you?'

'I did not,' she cried. 'I spent the evening talking to Rita.'

'Do you expect me to believe that?' His eyes were black.

'Yes,' she said. 'We were talking about men. We were saying how stupid they all were.'

Sadie went out with the girls the next day at lunch-time. She was fed up sitting in the cloakroom eating sandwiches on her own. She had had enough of being on her own in the evenings. After all, it wasn't as if she was an old married woman of thirty, she told herself. She spent less than the other girls, but even so, felt guilty at spending the money at all. She and Kevin had so little to spare. And she had the black dress to pay for at the end of the week. Her pay would only be half of what it should be. What would Kevin say?

'What's up with you?' asked Rita. 'You'd think there was poison in your soup.'

'It's not that.' Sadie stared at the pool of tomato-coloured liquid on her spoon. 'It's that dress. I don't know how I can pay for it.'

'Pay it up,' said Rita. 'A bit each week. That's what we all do. You can get more clothes that way.'

'Hi, girls!' Joe's voice made them turn.

Sadie spilled soup on her skirt. She scrubbed it with her handkerchief. The tomato colouring would leave a stain.

'How're you today, beautiful?' Joe caught a strand of her hair. She tossed her head, wincing with pain when he did not let go. 'Aren't you pleased to see me?'

'No.'

'He doesn't like girls who say no to him,' said Rita with a grin.

'He'll have to get used to it then,' said Sadie.

Joe pulled up a chair beside her and leaned his chin on her shoulder. 'No wonder they're all fighting one another where you come from,' he said. 'If they're all like you!'

'Did anyone ever tell you you're an eejit?' said Sadie, pushing his chin off her shoulder.

'No. But coming from you it sounds real cool. You've such a lovely way of saying it.'

'It takes a lot to get him riled,' said Rita.

Sadie wished Rita wouldn't grin all the time. Today she felt irritated by Rita with her false eyelashes and purple lips and her giggle. The trouble was that she felt irritated by everybody at present. By Kevin too.

'What in the name is this you've given me?' demanded Kevin when he looked at his dinner.

'Rissoles.'

'Rissoles. Tastes of bread.'

They were made mostly with bread and an egg and a small portion of sausage meat.

'I didn't have enough money to buy anything else,' Sadie snapped.

'But you had your housekeeping money this week.'

'Money goes nowhere these days,' she said, hearing echoes of her mother in her own voice. 'Food's a terrible price.'

'But even so.' Kevin forked amongst the drab-looking food. 'You can't expect a working man to eat this.'

'You can eat what you like. Or earn more money.'

Kevin laid down his knife and fork. 'Are you complaining then about my wages?'

'Only if you complain about my food.' Sadie swallowed the last of her rissole thinking it was the worst thing she could ever remember eating. She drank a cup of tea quickly to wash it down. 'Are you going out tonight?'

'I promised the lads I'd have a game of darts.'

'Great!'

'I'll stay at home if you want.'

'You sound dead keen.' She rose and lifted his plate.

'It's not that. But we've a match on Friday and we need the practice. Why don't you come and watch? Nobody would know you're not eighteen. You look it.'

'I feel eighty,' she said, scraping the remains off Kevin's plate into the litter bucket. 'Do you think I'd fancy sitting watching you playing darts?'

'I'll stay at home then.'

'And what'll we do? Sit and stare at one another?'

'What do you want then?' he asked.

She shrugged, having no answer. He turned on the radio and they listened to the news about Ulster. A soldier had been shot dead by a sniper, another was seriously ill. The incident had happened in a Catholic estate in Belfast.

'It's time they locked your lot up,' said Sadie.

'They're not my lot,' said Kevin angrily. He got up, switched off the radio. 'I might as well go out.'

She knew she had made the remark to annoy him. But he deserved it, she told herself, going out night after night leaving her alone, thinking only about himself. She paused a moment by the sink, frowning. She hated what was happening to them but could not seem to stop it. They were arguing about money; they were arguing about Ulster, and they had never argued about it before. When they lived there their revulsion at what was happening had brought them closer together. She sighed. She didn't want Rita to be proved right.

She put on her coat and walked along the street. Lights shone at windows. Families were at home eating their evening meals, talking to one another. Or were they? How did she know? Through many of the uncurtained windows she saw solitary figures eating off plates on their laps. A lot of people lived alone here, shut off in their separate rooms as if they were in boxes. A lot of people must be lonely.

She stopped outside the pub. It was a place of warmth where people went so that they would not be alone. Kevin was in there.

She pushed open the swing door and entered boldly. She need not have worried: no one paid any attention. The place was full of smoke. She stood inside the door, bemused by the chatter and the press of bodies. Then she saw Kevin's dark head standing up above the others. She stood on tiptoe, lifted her arm to wave to attract his attention. But as she lifted it her smile died and she lowered the arm again. Kevin was talking to two girls. She edged round a fat man to get a better view. Yes, there was Kevin, his face alight, listening to one of the girls as if what she had to say was of the greatest interest to him in the world. His shoulders crumpled and he laughed out loud, for all the pub and herself to hear.

She turned and walked out. As she walked she raged inside. He had lied to her, he hadn't gone out to play darts . . . The rage alternated with grief. She had lost him. What would she do with herself now? Crawl back to Belfast and tell her mother, 'He walked out on me.'? And then the anger returned again. If he wanted to spend his evenings in the pub talking to other girls instead of her he wasn't worth having!

She found herself on the tube. She went to Rita's without thinking. Rita was making up her face ready to go out. She sat at the mirror fixing on her eyelashes listening whilst Sadie recounted the tale of Kevin and his treachery.

'Told you, didn't I, duckie?' Rita wiggled the lashes to make sure they were firm.

'What am I going to do?' wailed Sadie.

'Come to the disco with us. Enjoy yourself. Have a good time. Forget him.'

'I can't go like this.' Sadie looked down at the reddish stain on her skirt.

'I'll lend you something.' Rita raked amongst the clothes in her wardrobe taking out several things on their hangers and holding them against Sadie. 'Not your colour. Too wide. What about this?' She held out a long purple dress decorated with gold braid.

'All right,' said Sadie.

She put it on and Rita exclaimed with admiration. It was just the thing for Sadie.

'You can have it,' she said.

'Not to keep,' said Sadie.

'Why not? I never wear it now. I only wear something a few times and then I get fed up with it.'

She did Sadie's hair, backcombing it and arranging it in elaborate swirls round her ears. Then she made up Sadie's face, covering the area round the eyes with several colours, finally fixing on a pair of false eyelashes. With them on Sadie felt a blinkered horse. She sat passively, allowing Rita to take her over and make her into whatever she wanted.

'I feel like Cinderella going to the ball,' giggled Sadie.

'Wait till Joe sees you!'

'Joe?'

'Yeh. He'll be there.'

He was. He swooped upon Sadie immediately. She allowed herself to be gathered up. She felt like a different person. The real Sadie had been left behind with her old clothes. Now she went through the motions of being a girl in a purple dress with false eyelashes and crimson lips with the feeling that she was looking on, that she was not really there. She took a glass when she was given it and drank. The liquid scalded her throat, warmed her stomach, went to her head. She drank another glass. She began to giggle, to lean on Joe's shoulder. He pulled her closer to him.

'I knew you'd give in,' he murmured.

The tempo of the music increased, the lights whirled in the room, Sadie's head spun like a top. She pushed Joe away from her.

'Back in a minute,' she muttered.

She went to the ladies' room. Sweat broke out on her forehead. She stood in the small cubicle steadying herself with one hand against the clammy wall. The floor tilted. And then she was sick.

Afterwards, she stood with her back against the wall, her head up. She breathed deeply, feeling the beat of her heart return to normal. The cloakroom was empty. She was thankful that Rita had not followed her. She looked in the mirror and saw that she was death-white. She pulled off the eyelashes feeling them tug at her own underneath. She did not care now, she did not care about anything except to get home to Kevin. She splashed water over her face scooping it from under the running tap into her cupped hands. The cold made her skin tingle; the sensation of being alive was gradually returning. The roller towel was grubby. She dried her face round the edge of it. When she looked in the mirror again she laughed: the make-up had run and she was a terrible looking sight!

She put on her coat, opened the door cautiously. No one was about. The noise boomed out from the discotheque. She scurried along the corridor, passed the doorman and was out in the street. The night was cold and fresh and stars streaked the sky above the rooftops. The fresh air felt good.

People stared at her on the tube but she did not care. She was going home. Home to Kevin.

When she came out of the station she picked up her skirts and ran all the way to their street. She was breathless when she reached their house. The light was on: he was home.

For a moment she stood in the porch calming the rapid gulps of breath. The felt-slippered woman shuffled along the corridor, holding something in her arms.

'One of my cats has died,' said the woman, showing Sadie the dead cat.

'Oh, I'm sorry,' said Sadie.

'Mrs Kyrakis said to put it in the dustbin. She's got no soul that woman. I'm going to bury him.'

'But there's no soil round here,' said Sadie. At the back of the house there was only a concrete yard.

'I'm taking him to the nearest park,' said the woman.

'Will they let you bury him there?'

'I don't care if they won't let me. I'm going to.'

The woman shuffled out into the night, in her slippers, her cat in her arms. Sadie watched her go thinking how terrible it was that so many people should be alone. Then she faced the door and turned the handle.

Kevin sat on the edge of the bed. His face was set, his eyes dark.

'Kevin!' she cried. 'I'm so glad to be home.'

'What have you got on?' He looked at the dress.

'It's Rita's.'

'And your face!'

'I was sick, you see, and then I washed it –'

'You look as if you've been sick.' His voice was hard and curt. 'You look like a tart!'

Chapter Twelve

She hated him. She stood with her back against the door staring at him and hating him. She had never imagined it would be possible that she would come to hate him. Anger coiled inside her like a snake.

'What did you call me?' she asked.

'A tart,' he said, looking her full in the eye.

'You've a queer nerve on you! Fenian git!' She spat the words out at him. They came from the centre of her where they had lain for years. 'Dirty ould pape!'

He sprang up, seized her by the shoulders.

'Take that back or I'll –'

'You'll what?' Her lip curled.

'I'll walk out of here and never come back.' He dropped his hands from her shoulders and walked to the window. He pulled back the curtain and stood looking out into the street. Now she felt afraid. If he had been angry and shaken her or screamed insults back at her she could have coped with it better. Once he would have given vent to his anger. When she had first met him he had been like that, ready to fight. But he had changed.

Why did he have to stand at that window with his back half-turned to her? Why didn't he look her in the eye? She liked to fight face to face. She should have stayed at the discotheque. She could have been laughing and dancing and enjoying herself.

She could have had Rita and the other girls to talk to and giggle with. She could have had Joe's arms round her.

'I don't know why I bothered coming home,' she said. 'Not to a sour-faced ould git like you!'

'I don't know why you bothered coming home either.'

'You'd just as soon I hadn't, wouldn't you?'

He did not answer her. She moved restlessly about the other end of the room. She caught sight of herself in the little mirror above the sink. Blotched eyes, streaks of black down her cheeks. She did not care.

'I can always go back to Rita's,' she said.

'Go if you want.'

She did not want to: that was the trouble. The thought of crawling into Rita's flat at this hour of the morning . . .

It was raining. Little slivers of water were running down the window. He watched one run from the top to the bottom.

'*You* can go if you want,' she said. 'It's nothing to me.'

He said nothing. He heard the water running in the sink. She was washing her face. A cat came padding quietly by on all fours not paying any attention to the rain. Now Sadie was cleaning her teeth. Each sound was familiar to him. He liked to lie in bed and watch her clean her teeth. She did it thoroughly, her whole body moving as she brushed.

'Well, what are you waiting for?' she said.

She began to brush her hair. The hair crackled under the bristles.

The rain was thickening. The slivers turned to a sheet of water washing over the pane shrouding the room from the street.

'Have you lost your tongue?' she asked.

'It's raining,' he said.

'You'll get wet then, won't you?

The bed springs creaked.

'If you're going to stand there all night you can put the light out,' she said. 'I'm wanting to go to sleep.'

The springs twanged as she turned over. He looked round now and saw her lying in the centre of the bed, her body

85

curled, her head on the pillow with her hands beside it, her eyes closed. He stood and looked at her in silence. One of her eyelids lifted, quickly dropped again. His mouth twitched. She began to breathe deeply as if to suggest sleep. She looked like a child with her freshly brushed hair and clean face. And yet she was not.

'You don't look like a tart at all,' he said.

She opened the eye fully, kept it open.

'I was just mad at you for coming in late,' he said. 'I thought you might be out with that Joe guy.'

She sat up, both eyes fully open now. 'Kevin –' she bit her lip. 'I was dancing with him. But I didn't go to the disco with him, honest I didn't. I went with Rita.'

Kevin felt his throat tightening. 'But you knew you'd see him there?'

'Yes but –'

'But nothing. You knew you'd see him. And you got dressed up and –'

'It was only because I saw you in the pub with those two girls,' she cried, cutting across him.

'Those two girls? You came into the pub? But I was only talking to them.'

'You looked as if you were enjoying yourself rightly,' she said, tossing her hair back over her shoulders. 'You were laughing like a drain.'

'There's nothing wrong with laughing is there?'

'Depends.'

She caught a thread in the bed cover and twisted it round her finger. She stared down at the thread cutting into her flesh. She pulled it tighter and watched the blood come and go in her finger.

He took two steps nearer her. 'You were jealous of me, were you?'

'You were jealous of Joe?'

'Yes.'

She looked up. Her eyes were wide and green. He sat down on the edge of the bed.

'Sadie, I don't want to go anywhere.'

Suddenly her arms were around him and he felt her wet tears on his neck

'I thought you did,' she said.

'I'd never leave you.'

'Never?'

He promised her.

'I'm sorry I called you all those names.' Now she was half laughing and half crying. 'You say terrible things to one another in a row, don't you?'

'You do that,' he said.

As usual he was asleep before she was, in a deep, sound sleep that would last until the alarm bell rang. She lay on her back, wide awake, listening to the rise and fall of his breathing. It had almost been the end of them. It frightened her to think it could have happened so easily. She did not understand how it was so easy one minute to love someone so much that it almost hurt and, the next, hate him more than she had ever hated anyone in her life. She must ask Lara. But Lara would only smile. She would never admit to hating Krishna.

Sadie slept fitfully, dreaming of Lara and Krishna and Orangemen marching and starving children. She awoke before Kevin, slipped out of bed and switched on the fire and radio. It was bitter cold in the room, a cold that entered her bones and made her shiver. Her head felt like lead and her stomach was on fire. She scurried back into bed again waking Kevin when she put her cold feet on his.

'Ouch!' He stretched and yawned.

They listened to the news. Another night of violence in Belfast. Bombs, fires, people fleeing for safety. Sadie sighed.

'And there were we fighting last night,' she said. 'We've little to trouble us compared with them.'

87

'You're right,' he said. 'It makes you see how stupid we can be.'

He sprang out of bed saying Siberia couldn't be any worse than this. She lifted her head from the pillow and let it sink back again.

'Are you all right?' he asked. 'Your face is the colour of the sheet.'

'I feel as if I've the 'flu,' she said weakly.

'You'll have to stay in bed then.' He tucked the blanket round her shoulder.

She hated lying in bed, had never been able to stand it. Long hours dragging by . . . She tried to sit up.

'Lie down!' said Kevin. 'And I'll make you a cup of tea.'

'All right,' she agreed weakly. Her strength seemed to have drained away during the night, and when Kevin gave her the cup her hand trembled and tea slopped on the bed covers. 'I really feel quite bad,' she said.

'You're going to be a few days off work by the looks of you.'

A few days. To lie here alone listening to the sounds of the street. At home there would have been neighbours and her mother coming in and out. She had never spent so much time on her own until she came to London.

Chapter Thirteen

Sadie tossed and turned, shivered and sweated, slept and dreamt. She dreamt of Orangemen marching in their dark suits and bowler hats, carrying their banners, their sashes gleaming orange and purple and gold. The bands played, drums banging deep and loud, the flutes tootling thin and high. They were marching, marching two abreast, keeping step; they were coming to fetch her for marrying a pape . . .

She awoke in a heavy sweat, her pyjamas sticking to her skin, the sheets damp around her, her hair heavy and matted on the pillow. The light in the room was grey: the day must have worn on into late afternoon.

She lay on her back, clammy now in the dampness, weak and exhausted.

'Kevin,' she called in a little voice that did not seem to be hers, but he did not answer. He was at work of course. He was never here when she needed him.

The house was quiet: most of the tenants would be at work. Someone was shuffling about the passage. Children played outside screaming and yelling. She was glad of the sound of the children.

Kevin came when the room was in dusk and light shone in the street. He put on the light over her head and she winced for it hurt her eyes.

'Sadie!' he cried. 'You're really ill. I'll have to get the doctor.'

'We haven't got one,' she said.

'There must be one round about.'

She was too limp to bother. She allowed him to help her change her pyjamas and the sheets and then she lay back exhausted again. He looked so worried that she caught his hand and smiled at him.

'Don't worry,' she said, and fell asleep.

But he was worried. It was terrible to see Sadie, usually so full of life, felled so quickly and thoroughly. Her fever was running high, her breath laboured. Illness worried him, and frightened him.

Mrs Kyrakis opened her door after he had knocked insistently for five minutes.

'My wife is ill,' he began.

'Ill?' She looked suspicious.

'Just 'flu I think.'

'You think?' She tugged her skirt round her fat stomach to straighten it. An inch of greyish underskirt showed below. She was frowning heavily. 'I hope not anything infectious. I have many lodgers to consider.'

'Oh, not infectious,' said Kevin. 'I just wondered if you could tell me where to get a doctor.'

'You find one on the main road near the shops.' She closed the door.

Kevin ran to the main road, saw the doctor's brass plate at once. He went into the house and explained the situation to the receptionist.

'If you're not Dr Bell's patients –' She shook her head.

'But we're not anybody's patients,' said Kevin desperately.

'Where are you registered?'

'In Belfast. But surely –'

'I could ask Dr Bell to call tomorrow,' said the woman.

'Can't he come this evening?'

'I'm afraid not. He's a very busy man, he has a surgery this evening and the waiting room is full of patients.'

'Never mind,' said Kevin wearily. 'I'll see if I can get someone else.'

He walked home slowly.

At home his family doctor would have come straight away. No one cared in London. You could be dying ... Of course Sadie could not be dying. He began to run.

A light shone from Lara's window. She was sitting in the room with her husband watching television. Krishna answered the door to Kevin's knock.

'My wife's ill,' said Kevin, 'and I don't know what to do.'

'Ill?' said Lara's voice behind Krishna.

'Yes, she's got a terrible fever,' said Kevin. 'I'm right worried about her.'

Lara joined Krishna at the door. Her eyes were concerned.

'You had better come in,' said Krishna.

The invitation was so unexpected that it was a second or so before Kevin realized that he was actually being asked to come in. He stepped inside their room and Krishna closed the door behind him. The room smelled of curry and other spices. He saw that they too had to cook and live in the same room.

'Please sit down,' said Lara as graciously as if she lived in a silken drawing room.

'Thank you,' he said.

The springs had gone in the chair he was offered, just like their own chairs. But the room was bright. Lara had hung Indian prints against the walls and over the chairs. The baby slept in a cot at the far end with a screen around him. On a table stood a pile of books and loose leaf folders.

'Krishna is studying,' said Lara. 'He wants to become a teacher.'

'And then we will move to a real house,' said Krishna.

Lara smiled at him. Then she asked Kevin about Sadie.

'You could go and look at her, Lara,' said Krishna, and to Kevin added, 'Lara is a trained nurse.'

'Would you come?' asked Kevin eagerly.

Lara rose. 'Of course.'

Lara and Kevin went to Sadie. She was still tossing and turning and moaning in her sleep.

'Those drums!' she cried.

'Drums?' Lara looked at Kevin.

'It's the drums in Belfast.'

'Ah!' Lara nodded. She put her slender hand on Sadie's brow and frowned.

'Is she bad, do you think?' asked Kevin.

'Not good,' said Lara, now becoming very brisk. 'If you could give me a clean towel I will sponge her down and try to lower the temperature.'

He had a job to find a clean towel: they were short of towels. They were short of everything. Lara understood. She said a semi-clean one would do very well. She took a bowl of tepid water and began to sponge Sadie with it. Sadie opened her eyes and frowned.

'It's me, Lara,' said Lara softly. When she finished the sponging, she gave Sadie some water to drink. 'She needs plenty of liquids, Kevin.'

Kevin nodded.

'Evening class, Kevin,' said Sadie thickly.

'Sure I'm not going to that tonight,' he said. 'I'm staying here to look after you.' To Lara he said quietly, 'What do you think then, Lara?'

'I'm worried about her temperature. It would be better to have a doctor look at her.'

'But where will we get one?'

'We have a friend who is a doctor. I'm sure he would come. I will go and ask Krishna to telephone him.'

Kevin sat beside Sadie whilst Lara went next door. Her hand in his was hot and she was thrashing around in the bed like a wounded animal.

'My head,' she said. 'It's going to lift off.'

He stroked her brow, pushing the damp hair back from it. Lara was right: her temperature was very high.

A few minutes later Krishna came to say that their friend was on his way.

'Thank you very much,' said Kevin.

'A pleasure,' said Krishna, with a small bow.

His friend arrived soon. Kevin saw the car stop outside.

'The doctor is come, Sadie,' he told her.

The doctor's name was Dr Menon. He too was Indian, in his twenties, a plump bustling little man with white teeth that showed every time he smiled.

'Well, well, what have we here?' he asked, rubbing his hands. 'We will have you dancing up the street in no time, young lady.'

He hummed slightly to himself as he examined Sadie. He examined her thoroughly. He winked at her when he saw her watching him so seriously.

'You will not die yet,' he said.

'Good.'

'You think life is good?'

Sadie nodded.

Kevin smiled at her. He looked at the bare, dirty-fawn wall behind her head and thought that one day they would have their own house and everything in it would be bright and new. He would buy her some flowers tomorrow. Yellow chrysanthemums. He had passed some standing in a bucket outside a shop that day.

'Now then, Sadie,' said Dr Menon, 'you have to be a good girl and do what I say. You stay in bed and take the medicine that I give you and drink a lot. Isn't that easy? And I will come back to see you tomorrow.'

He gave Kevin a prescription and also a bottle of medicine for Sadie to start taking straightaway.

'I am very grateful,' began Kevin but Dr Menon brushed his thanks aside.

'What am I a doctor for?' he demanded.

'What a nice man!' said Sadie, after he had gone.

She slept restlessly that night; Kevin did not sleep at all. He stayed up all night wiping her head, giving her drinks, talking to her when she wanted him to. In the morning she was cooler and quieter. He left her sleeping and set off to work.

She awoke to find that it was full daylight. There was even a hint of winter sunshine in the room. 'Kevin,' she called, but he was not there. He had been there all night though: that she remembered. His hand had been cool and firm against her head. Her body was damp again but more comfortable. Her limbs ached but she was more at peace.

She was pleased to see Lara when she came in. She was wearing a deep pink sari. She glided smoothly round the room beneath the shimmering colour and when she moved Sadie smelt her perfume, light and aromatic.

'You look lovely, Lara,' said Sadie, nodding with approval.

'And you look much better,' said Lara. 'I can stay a few minutes whilst the baby is sleeping.'

Dr Menon arrived soon afterwards.

'What's this?' he said. 'A social gathering? And my patient is lying there smiling when last night she was trying to pretend she was at death's door.'

He and Lara talked to one another with much laughing and joking. They came from the same province in India, had come over to London about the same time. He had married a friend of Lara's, another nurse.

'I think you are on the mend,' he said to Sadie.

'Sure I think you're right,' said Sadie.

'But you must stay in bed. I shall come again tomorrow.'

Sadie was content that day to lie in bed. The weakness in her body made even standing difficult but next day she felt a little better again and began to be restless. Lara visited her, bringing soup and two books from the library.

'I don't read much,' said Sadie. 'When I was a kid I was always running about the streets.'

'Why don't you try?' suggested Lara.

Sadie read one of the books after Lara went away.

'I enjoyed it,' she said with surprise to Kevin at tea-time. 'It was a good story. I think I might take up reading.'

Kevin smiled.

On Wednesday, the shop's half-day, Rita and Sally called.

'We thought we'd better make sure you were still living,' said Rita, throwing herself into one of the armchairs. She looked round the room. 'Blimey, what a place! Couldn't you get yourself anything better than this?'

'No,' said Sadie. 'We'd no money when we arrived in London and Kevin's not making much at his job.'

Sally yawned. 'I'm dead today. We were out last night, didn't get in till four.'

'It was murder getting up for work this morning.' Rita grinned. 'Joe sent you his love.'

'He can keep it,' said Sadie. 'I'm not interested.'

Rita and Sally stayed till Kevin came home. Sadie thought that they would, they were curious to see him. She did not mind: she enjoyed having them there, chatting and laughing, full of stories of the outside world, a world that she felt cut off from.

'Nice meeting you,' said Rita to Kevin. She eyed him up and down, obviously with approval.

'It's nice to meet you too,' said Kevin.

'See you soon, Sadie,' called the girls. 'Ta-ta for now.' They were going home to get ready for a party.

'What did you think of them?' asked Sadie after they had clattered past the window.

'Not much,' said Kevin.

'What do you mean?' cried Sadie. 'They're all right. They're my friends –'

'Hey! Your temperature will go up.' He grinned. 'And we

haven't had a row since the night before you were ill. Don't let's break the record.'

Sadie subsided. Kevin cooked the meal. He was getting handier in the kitchen, she told him. He made a face and said he didn't fancy himself as a housewife. Sadie stretched her toes in contentment.

'Life is O.K.,' she said.

She recovered rapidly though Dr Menon would not let her go back to work until she was completely fit. It did not matter whether she missed a few days at work, he said, no one would collapse because of it.

'We are not all that important,' he said. 'Except to ourselves.'

'And the people we live with,' said Sadie.

'That's true!'

When he had gone she went to see Lara. Now Lara asked her to come in when she called. Krishna had accepted them, said Lara, he had just needed time.

Today Lara said, 'I am going to have a little dinner party on Saturday evening. Dr Menon and his wife are coming to visit us and Krishna and I would be pleased if you and Kevin would join us too. We will be having an Indian dinner. Would you like that?'

'Like it?' Sadie's eyes shone. She threw her arms around Lara's neck. 'Oh Lara, how marvellous!'

Lara laughed. 'You would think I was giving you a hundred pounds. It will not be that grand.'

'But you see,' said Sadie, 'it's the first time Kevin and I have ever been invited out together since we were married.'

Chapter Fourteen

Lara's dinner party was a success. Sadie and Kevin enjoyed the food, even though the curry burnt their throats and almost brought tears to their eyes. They had been determined to enjoy it. They drank several glasses of water.

'You'll get used to it in time,' said Dr Menon.

He was jolly and full of fun. He and Lara laughed a lot. His wife was quieter and did not smile so much. Her face was pock-marked; she was not as pretty as Lara, but her sari was beautiful, flame-orange. Sadie sighed, and said she wished that she was Indian and could wear saris. That amused Lara. Alina, Dr Menon's wife just looked at Sadie with mild eyes. Krishna was quiet but agreeable, allowing Dr Menon and Lara to do most of the talking. He sat with his long thin fingers linked round his knee listening, nodding, contributing sometimes.

Back in their own room, drinking a cup of tea to slake their thirst before going to bed, Sadie talked over the evening happily. She speculated on Alina and Krishna, discussing every aspect of the evening.

'You'd think Lara would have been better married to Dr Menon,' she said. 'They seem better suited.'

'Who can tell?' said Kevin. 'Perhaps they need someone different. Like you and I.'

'Are we different?'

'In many ways.'

'Oh, religion and all that –'

'All that makes people different.' He smiled. 'Come on, let's go to bed.'

97

Sadie went to bed and dreamt of herself floating around in saris of all colours of the rainbow. It was a happy dream until the drums started to bang and the flutes to play and then she awoke in a sweat.

'It's the curry that gave you indigestion,' said Kevin.

'But why do I keep dreaming about drums and Orange parades? And every time Father Mulcahy calls I'm sure to dream of them afterwards.'

Kevin shrugged. 'We can't get away from Ireland all that easily.'

'If you didn't put on the news every half-hour of the day we might forget it.'

'How can we turn a deaf ear to what's going on?'

Kevin listened avidly to the news broadcasts, Sadie tried to ignore them. She knew Kevin was apprehensive about his family: they lived in one of the most troublesome areas in Belfast, they were a large family and his father had brothers and sisters with large families, and it seemed only a matter of time until one of them stopped a bullet or was blown up by a bomb. Her family was safer for there was less trouble in the Protestant streets, but no one was really safe anywhere in the city. Every day a bomb exploded in a shop, pub, or an office building. It hung over their heads like a black cloud.

'We would worry less if we were there,' said Kevin.

'You're not suggesting we go back? We've been through all that.'

'No, I'm not suggesting that.'

Letters from home were ripped open at once and quickly scanned for reports of disaster.

'Brian Rafferty's been arrested,' said Kevin, looking up from a letter from Brede. Brian Rafferty lived in the same street and they had played together as boys.

'Serves him right, doesn't it?' said Sadie.

'If he's guilty,' said Kevin. 'A man's innocent till he's proved otherwise.'

'Oh, you make me sick! You know full well Brian Rafferty was mixed up with the Provos. Didn't he show you a gun under his bed and then framed you so that you got the blame for it?'

'Aye, but still –'

'Still what? He and two of his pals beat you up for going out with me didn't they?'

'Yes, they did,' said Kevin.

They had beaten him up and he had beaten Rafferty in return and sickened himself of violence. Walking to work he thought of it. He had had Rafferty's blood on his hands. Their marriage had been born out of bloodshed and trouble. Because of them too, a man had died, a good kind man who had befriended and helped them. Was it right to let your own happiness cause such misery to others? And yet, if they had given in, it would have been like giving in to all of it, the prejudice and hate, the violence and stupidity.

'What's up with you this morning, lad?' asked Mr Davis.

'Nothing.'

Kevin sat down at the bench, took up a screwdriver. He was working on a radio. He enjoyed his work, the satisfaction of taking something so intricate apart, fixing it, putting it back together again and seeing that it worked. His fingers moved deftly, each week becoming surer and surer. As he worked he dreamt of owning his own shop one day.

'Trouble at home?' asked Mr Davis.

'There's always trouble.'

'Aye, lad,' Mr Davis sighed. 'You just have to live with it.'

Kevin nodded. They lived with it over there, still going about their daily lives, shopping, working, going to school. You couldn't sit at home cringing with fear for what might happen.

Kevin finished the radio, screwed the back into place, turned on the sound. Music poured out.

'You're doing well, Kevin,' said Mr Davis. 'You've caught

on fast. I was thinking it would be a good thing for you to have some driving lessons. It would be a help if you could drive the van. I'll pay for half of them. I couldn't afford to pay the lot.'

'Driving lessons are dear,' said Sadie with a sigh when Kevin told her. 'But I suppose you'll have to have them.'

'It'd be fine and handy to be able to drive, Sadie. It means there's other jobs I could do if the telly business went down.'

Sadie make stovies that night: potatoes cooked with fat and onions, a real Irish dish, a dish for people who had to live on the minimum of money.

'Sure it tastes good,' declared Kevin, wiping his plate with bread. 'I was brought up on them.'

'I wasn't,' said Sadie. 'Me ma said it was for potato pickers. We had stew and ham and eggs.'

'You came from a good Protestant working-class family, don't forget!' said Kevin good-naturedly. 'They were always better off than the Catholic working class. They were in work more often.'

'And they had fewer kids to feed,' retorted Sadie.

They grinned at one another. They could argue again without bitterness, as it had been in the old days.

Kevin set off for his evening class feeling contented. His stomach was full of savoury potatoes and he was less worried about Sadie. She had perked up again, she was very friendly with Lara and had found a young girl further along the street who had just arrived from Sheffield and was lonely. Sadie invited the girl in for coffee a couple of evenings a week and they sat together and sewed.

Sadie had also struck up a street friendship with an old man who walked his dog up and down the pavement every hour on the hour. The old man lived alone and was almost blind, and no one ever came to visit him. He had four sons whom he had not seen for ten years, which outraged Sadie. She fumed against them to Kevin. Whenever the old man was ill she called at his house and went shopping for him and made him a cup of tea. He had once been in the navy and had tales to tell of life on the high seas. Kevin smiled to himself. Sadie was making inroads on the street. She said good morning persistently to everyone she passed. It would not be long before she knew them all. She needed people, neighbours, contact in the street, more than he did. She was beginning to settle.

'London is not so bad,' he said to her as they walked on Hampstead Heath one Sunday.

'Not so bad,' she said. She pointed across the heath. 'What about that house? The one with the big garden on the corner. One day when you have your own shop . . .'

Chapter Fifteen

When the telegram came, they felt no surprise. It was as if they had been awaiting it, as if it had only been a matter of time; and yet, strangely, it was totally unexpected, for bad things in life seem always to happen to other people.

Sadie took the little yellow envelope from the post office boy. It was such a small flimsy envelope that it could scarcely contain any news of importance. But the yellow colour was ominous. She could only remember a few times as a child when a telegram arrived. Each time it had been bad news. Her granny had died, an aunt was seriously ill. If news was good people wrote letters and did not waste their money. The post office boy picked up his bicycle from the gutter and rode off.

'Sadie?' Kevin called from within the house.

'Yes?'

'What are you doing out there, for dear sake?'

'Nothing.'

She continued to stand on the step looking at the envelope. Mr Kevin McCoy, the name said. She was afraid. Afraid to go in and give it into his hands and watch him open and read it and see the hurt in his eyes.

The old man with the dog went past on the other side of the street. He held up his stick in greeting; she waved back automatically. The world was moving just as it always did.

'Are you going to stand there all day?' Kevin came up behind her, put his hands round her waist and squeezed her.

'There must be something desperately interesting going on in the street to keep you out here gawping!'

She crushed the telegram against her side. She could not bear to have him hurt. He rocked her a little, keeping his arms round her.

'What'll we do the day?' he said. 'Sure isn't it fine when you don't have to go to work?' It was one of Sadie's Saturdays off.

She closed her eyes, leant back against him.

'Hey, what's up with you?' He turned her round, saw that she held something in her hand. 'What is it? Who was it at the door asking for us?'

She held up the telegram. He took it from her. They went into their room together and closed the door.

He sat down on the bed. She stood near him, her eyes large, fixed on his face, as he slowly slit open the envelope and removed the small piece of paper. He read the message, his lips moving soundlessly.

'My da's dead,' he said then. 'Killed. By a bomb in a pub.'

She sat down beside him, not touching him. He passed her the telegram and she read it for herself so that she would believe it. It had been sent by Brede.

'He must have gone for a drink,' said Kevin. 'He often did in the evening. And the bomb went off.'

'Yes,' said Sadie. Her lips felt stiff and dry.

'It happens all the time,' said Kevin.

'Yes,' said Sadie.

'My da always had plenty to say,' said Kevin. 'He was always sounding off but he never would have harmed a man.'

'No,' said Sadie. She had not met him and now never would.

Kevin read the telegram again. It said so little and yet so much.

'I shall have to go home,' he said.

'Of course,' said Sadie, knowing that she would not be able to go with him and stand by his side and give comfort to him and Brede and his mother. She would have to stay here wondering and waiting. All her life she had hated waiting.

'My mother will need me,' said Kevin.

'Brede too.'

Kevin was the man of his family now, the eldest son. There were so many small children, needing care and attention. Some of the boys ran wild, causing great concern to their mother.

'I suppose you could always go over too and see your family,' said Kevin, but Sadie shook her head. It would not be the right time for that and besides, they had only enough money for Kevin's fare and she would have to keep her job.

'I'll take night boat from Liverpool,' said Kevin.

There were things to do. He went out and sent a telegram to Brede to say that he was coming, and he found out the time of the trains from Euston Station. These were practical, necessary things that kept his body functioning. On the way back he went into the church to light a candle and say a prayer for his father's soul. Whilst he was gone Sadie ironed his two shirts and packed his suitcase.

She cooked him a meal. He ate very little even though she tried to coax him saying that he had a long journey ahead and he would have a lot to do when he arrived home. His face was pale, his eyes dark; he had gone in spirit from the room, was already in the kitchen of his house where his mother would be sitting with the neighbours coming and going bringing sympathy and gifts of food.

It was Sadie who wept before he left. He patted her shoulder and let her cry against him.

'You'll be all right whilst I'm gone, won't you?' he said. 'I'll write and let you know how things are going on. And you'll go and see Mr Davis and tell him I'll be back as soon as I can?'

She did not dare to ask how long that would be. He did not know himself.

'Take care of yourself,' she said, her throat rough. She was thinking now of his safety, for he was going back into a Catholic area where many people would resent that he had married a Protestant girl.

'You don't have to worry about me.'

He kissed her and then he went, walking quickly, looking back only once. The room was empty, as empty as if he had been gone a long time. She could hardly believe he had stood here a few minutes before. She shivered, cold right to the middle of her body, remembering the cold she felt when their friend Mr Blake had been killed. Death makes you cold, she thought. She put on Kevin's thick rough sweater. It smelt of him, comforted her a little. She sat before the fire rocking herself, wishing she was with him. In death people gathered together, closed their ranks, reaffirmed their family ties. Kevin was gone to be with his family, his rightful place at such a time. They would feel close to one another, talk, weep, keep one another warm. Sadie ran her hands over the coarse wool, arching her shoulders inside the sweater.

'Kevin,' she said softly. 'Kevin.'

It was midday. The cheap clock they had bought when they first came said so. It stood on the mantelpiece between pictures of their families.

Midday on Saturday, and all the rest of the week-end stretched ahead.

She went next door and knocked at Lara and Krishna's room but there was no reply. Then she remembered that they were going to have lunch with the Menons. She wandered along the street and met the old man with the dog.

'My father-in-law has been killed by a bomb,' she told him. 'And Kevin's gone home.'

The old man shook his head. 'These are terrible times,' he said. 'People murdering one another.'

'I suppose times have always been as terrible,' said Sadie.

'And as good,' said the old man, surprising her for she did

not think that any part of his life could be called good, unless it was on account of his dog.

'Each day has something good in it,' he said.

She nodded. Meeting and talking to him was good, was no part of the terrible side.

'Will you come home and have some lunch with me?' she said. 'It'll only be beans on toast,' she added.

'I like beans on toast,' he replied.

They had quite a gay lunch. She could not understand it: Kevin's father was dead and the grief in her was real and yet she could sit and laugh with this old man and pat his dog and part of her was even happy. She tried to explain what she felt to Mr Dooley but he did not find it strange, he said. It was all part of life, he said, for even in a bad patch you found yourself thinking it was worth living.

'Kevin will come back to you. He'll have a hard time in between but he'll come back and you'll be happy together.'

'You're a very wise old man, Mr Dooley,' she said solemnly, and he laughed, for he had never been called wise before and would never have thought that he was. To end life alone in a room with a dog was not wise; it was not planned, it had happened.

'I've just lived a long time. That gives me some advantage over you. But not much. You're young, Sadie, that's a big thing.'

When he went home she fell asleep in front of the fire, exhausted.

She awoke, stiff and crumpled, in the dark room. Kevin would be in Liverpool now, waiting for the boat to carry him across the Irish Sea.

Chapter Sixteen

The crossing was stormy, in keeping with his mood. After the initial numbness, when he had seemed to feel very little, anger had taken over. Rain swept the deck of the ship, splashing against his face. He walked with his shoulders hunched, hands clenched inside his pockets, not caring whether he was soaked or borne over the side by the wind into the bucketing, dark water. No one else walked the deck; they slept in neat narrow berths or dozed open-mouthed in the stale atmosphere of the saloon. At least they did if they were not being sick. He almost wished that he could be sick, so that he would be absorbed by that, and not by the terrible pain in the middle of his chest. He had never known anything like it before.

His father was dead. And he wanted to kill the man who had put the bomb in that pub. He had trained himself not to fight every time he was riled. But this was different. His father had been murdered.

His father had died and he had had no chance to make peace with him before he died. They had parted on good terms in Belfast but when his father had heard of his marriage to Sadie he had written him a strong letter telling him he needn't bother his head about coming home as long as he had a Prod for a wife. If only his father had written to say, 'Never mind, son, I don't mind about your wife, bring her home and we'll take her in as part of our family.' But he hadn't written that and he never would have done. It ate into Kevin that his father had died with a feeling of bad blood between them. It was hard to bear, as well as the loss of his father himself.

Kevin spent the night on deck.

By morning the storm had blown itself out and they came up Belfast Lough in peace. He watched the boat slide through the calm water leaving a white ripple to mark its passage. He looked at the green shores of Antrim and Down on either side, soft and blurred in the early morning light, and a thrill surged through him. It was his own country. He was coming home.

He had not realised how homesick he had been during these months away. In their dingy London street they had remembered only the bad things of home, the fighting and burning and the desolate streets. But here there was land green and sweet: his native land.

His anger was spent. He did not want to kill the men who had planted the bomb. That way was a hopeless one: he knew it too well. He did not even want to know who the men were, whether they were Protestants bent on destroying a few Catholics or Catholics who had been keeping the bomb in the pub before they took it to put in a car or building to cause havoc and destruction.

When the boat docked he was impatient to leave. He was first to set foot on the gangway. He went down it quickly and hurried into the sheds, through the piles of cargo and the gathering people. Outside in the street his brothers Gerald and Michael were waiting for him. He slapped them on the back, put one arm on each shoulder. They had grown tall, would soon be men. Gerald was fifteen, Michael thirteen.

'Boys, it's great to see the two of you! You'll soon be as tall as me.'

'I leave school this year,' said Gerald.

'Sure he's hardly ever there as it is,' said Michael.

'I've other things to do,' said Gerald, and Kevin felt uneasy, having some idea of what those things might be. Gerald had always been fired with enthusiasm for the IRA.

'How's ma?' asked Kevin.

Gerald's face went dark. 'Poorly. We'll sort out those gits yet!'

They passed gutted buildings, patches of bare ground. Soldiers went by in trucks and on foot, walking warily with eyes shifting from side to side. When two had passed Gerald spat into the gutter.

'Fat lot of good that'll do,' said Kevin, and then he was quiet. It was not the time for arguing with Gerald. He allowed the boy to talk. He was full of boasts of what he had done.

'He's a Provo,' said Michael, glancing over his shoulder.

Kevin looked at his brother Gerald as if he was a stranger. He did not want a brother of his to be a killer.

'He helped tar and feather Kate Kelly,' said Michael with a giggle. 'Him and a crowd of women. Did you read about that over there?'

'Aye, I read about it and it made me want to boke!' said Kevin vehemently. 'Of all the stupid cowardly things –'

Gerald swung round and caught Kevin by the arms.

'Take that back or I'll lay you out!'

'I'll take nothing back. It's time you heard a thing or two, Gerald McCoy. You might think you're the big brave lad but you're the stupidest –'

Gerald lifted his right hand and punched Kevin in the mouth. Blood trickled from one side. For a moment the three brothers were still on the pavement. Michael giggled nervously.

Gerald stood defiantly, feet astride, eyes steady and hot, watching Kevin. Kevin took his handkerchief from his pocket, dabbed his lip, put it back. Then slowly he took hold of Gerald's arms. Gerald came to life struggling and wriggling. He kicked out catching Kevin on the shin. Fury surged through Kevin. He pushed Gerald against the wall and pinned him there, forcing his head back against the bricks. He was bigger and older than Gerald and much stronger too, with years of work in his arms. The younger boy was powerless. He gasped and spluttered.

'If you do that again I'll bash the brains out of you,' said Kevin. 'And if you tar and feather another girl I'll do the same.'

Then he pushed Gerald to one side. The boy fell on to one knee. He waited there for a moment looking down on the pavement before he got to his feet unsteadily.

'Let's go home now,' said Kevin. 'And remember that your father's dead and not even buried yet and the sight of two of her sons fighting would break your mother's heart.'

They walked in silence the rest of the way through the streets. Gerald walked with his head down. He would not be as easily squashed as he looked, Kevin knew. Kevin's heart was heavy at the thought that he and his brother had been fighting within an hour of his return home.

Brede met them at the door.

'Oh Kevin!' she cried putting her arms round his neck.

He hugged her, lifting her off her feet. Gerald pushed past them to go up the stairs.

'What's up with him?' asked Brede.

'He and I had a bit of a dispute, you might say.' Kevin touched his lip involuntarily.

'Did he do that?' Brede frowned. 'He's a wild one, Kevin, and I'm real worried about him. I don't know how he'll end up.'

'Is that you, Kevin?' His mother had opened the kitchen door and stood there waiting for him. She had aged. He went towards her.

'Sure it's me right enough, ma!'

She hugged him close to her, reluctant to let him go in case he might disappear. She wiped the tears from her eyes with the edge of her apron and made him sit by the fire in the kitchen whilst she and Brede cooked him a good breakfast of ham and eggs and fried potato bread.

'Kevin, I'm so pleased to have you home!'

'And I'm right pleased to be home.' He looked round at the old familiar kitchen, the small room in which his large family ate and his mother washed and ironed and cooked. She was looking ill: her face was drawn and the skin beneath her eyes was purple as if it had been bruised. The cream and red clock ticked on the dresser, and above it hung a replica of Christ on the Cross.

Kevin ate well for he had had little food for twenty-four hours and the long cold night on deck had left the life in his body lowered. His mother sat across the table drinking a cup of tea, watching him eat, each bite he took giving her pleasure. He would need all the energy he could get.

'You're the head of the family now, Kevin,' she said.

Kevin frowned down at his plate, not wanting to look her in the eye. He had eight younger brothers and sisters and a mother who were now his concern. And on the other side of the Irish Sea he had a wife of a different faith. He closed his eyes for a moment. It all seemed too much.

''Deed you must be tired after such a night,' cried Mrs McCoy. 'You'll be needing a lie down.'

'No, no,' he told her. 'I couldn't sleep. I don't want to lie down.'

Brede had made all the arrangements for the funeral. The neighbours and priest had helped them.

'What about Uncle Albert?' asked Kevin, for no mention had been made of him.

'Poor Albert,' sighed Mrs McCoy. 'He was with your da in the pub and he had a leg and an arm blown off him. I think it'd have been as well if he'd been taken.'

'Dear help us!' Kevin shook his head. So Uncle Albert would never tie up his old car with string again and set off on one of his famous journeys. He had loved going on journeys in his old car.

'He's lying in the hospital in a dreadful state,' said Mrs

McCoy. 'And your Aunty Patsy's in a terrible state and all, as you might imagine.'

'But you're not,' said Kevin.

'What's the point? I've the children to think of. I have to live on.'

His mother asked him about his life in London but did not mention Sadie, and neither did he. It was an odd conversation for his life in London meant Sadie. But instead he talked of his job and the business of the city and the unfriendliness of the people compared to the ones who lived in their own street.

'There's nothing to beat your own kind, Kevin,' sighed his mother.

When she went upstairs Brede asked about Sadie.

'She's fine,' said Kevin. 'She sent you her love and to tell you she was sorry about da.'

Brede smiled a little sadly. 'I wish all this trouble was over, Kev, and then you could bring her home.'

'Could I ever?' he demanded.

He got up from the table and went to stand by the sink looking out of the window at the small backyard and the brick wall behind it and then at the backs of the brick terraced houses in the next street. Nothing grew in the back yard except for a few weeds pushing determinedly up between the broken concrete.

'Kevin,' said Brede.

He turned round.

'I'm engaged,' she said shyly.

'That's great! Who's the lucky man?'

'A boy from Tyrone. He's called Robert. I met him down at Aunty May's.'

'Isn't that marvellous?' He whirled her round.

She said, 'But I don't know if I can marry him now.'

'Why ever not?'

'I was going to go and live in Tyrone. But how could I go and leave ma after what's happened?'

'But you can't give up your own chance, Brede,' said Kevin.

'Ma's not well.' Brede sighed. 'Her strength's never been the same since her operation. It's not had a chance to pick up with all the kids to look after. And Gerald's a terrible worry to her all the time.'

'And now da's gone,' said Kevin slowly, sitting down at the table again, 'she's on her own and not able.'

'She's worked hard all her life,' said Brede. 'Too hard.'

'Don't you do the same, Brede.' Kevin spoke urgently, for he had always seen Brede following in the image of their mother.

Brede shook her head. 'Times are changing, Kevin. My life'll never be like hers. I won't have nine kids and live in a dirty city street. I was going to –'

'Going to what?'

'Live in a cottage in the country.' She shrugged. 'That was all.'

'That was a lot. And you're still going to do it, Brede. You've got to!' Colour surged in Kevin's cheeks. He went on even more urgently, 'It'll be peaceful and quiet and you've always loved the country. I'll see to it that you get there. You've done your share for the family. You've been the one to get landed with all the jobs, stay at home and look after the kids. I remember you cooking the dinner when you were only as high as the stove when ma was in hospital having one of the babies.'

When he stopped speaking Brede gave him a small smile. Her eyes were sad. She knew it was true that she had had to do much for the family, she had had little chance of childhood and had not minded for it had all seemed to be natural and expected, but she did not believe it when Kevin told her that she would still go to Tyrone and live in the little farm worker's cottage and keep a few hens and plant flowers around the door. And each night Robert would come back from work with his boots thick with mud, his face ruddy from sun and wind, and she would –

'It can't be,' she said.

'Yes, it can. I will look after them now. After all, it's my place to. As ma said, I'm the head of the family.'

'But you've got Sadie,' said Brede.

Chapter Seventeen

Sadie read Kevin's letter for the third time. It was not that it said much but it was all the contact that she had with him. He had written it two days ago on cheap blue lined paper.

He said that his mother was not at all well and he was worried about her, and that Gerald was wild and he was worried about him, and Brede was engaged to be married and he was worried about her for she said that now she could not get married. He did not say that he was worried about Sadie left alone in London. At once Sadie was ashamed of her thought. Indeed she was glad that he had not said he was worried about her for he had faith that she could fend for herself and survive.

By now his father would be buried. But Kevin had not said when he would be coming back. He had ended the letter, 'Love Kevin' and two crosses. The word love looked awkward as if he had found it difficult to write. But he did love her. Of course he did!

'Dear help us!' she said aloud. 'I'll be going round the twist if I start imagining things.'

Her meal, two frozen hamburgers and a grilled tomato, had grown cold whilst she was reading. She pushed the plate aside and took out a pad of writing paper.

'Dear Kevin', she wrote. And then she stopped and bit the end of the biro pen. Neither of them was much good when it came to writing letters. 'I am missing you.' No, she could not write that for he might feel guilty and think he ought to rush back at once. But she wanted him to rush back. 'I am sorry that your mother is not well', she wrote. 'And that Gerald is so wild. It must be a big worry for you. Tell Brede that she must get married.' Sadie stopped. Tell Brede that she must get married? What was so great about being married when you were only seventeen years old and had to spend half the time sitting in a grotty room with no money to buy clothes or go out and have a good time? Maybe she should cross that out and put instead, 'Tell Brede that she has plenty of time to get married in.' She scribbled on the inside cover of the writing pad. What else could she say to him? 'I had a boring awful day at work. Miss Cullen was in a bad mood and scowled at everybody. The girls were all giggling about a party they had been to last night. I am fed up sitting in this room and don't think I can stand it much longer. Love Sadie.' She grinned. That might bring him back. But of course she would not write it.

She sighed, got up, stretched herself and went to the window. It was dark in the street but most of the windows of the houses were lit. She had another evening to fill and not even Kevin to come back at the end of it to give her a kiss and ruffle her hair with his hand. She could go along and visit Mr Dooley but she had done that last night. Some boys went past on the pavement laughing and jostling one another. She returned to her letter.

'Don't worry about me,' she wrote. 'I am all right. I have been to see Mr Davis and he says not to worry and he is sorry about your dad. Love Sadie.' She added ten kisses and then folded the page and put it in an envelope. She found a stamp in her purse. At least now she had a reason to go out.

She took a roundabout route to the nearest letter box so that her journey would not pass too quickly. On her way back she came by the Catholic church. Father Mulcahy stood outside talking to a woman.

'Ah Sadie!' he called.

Sadie paused. She waited whilst the priest said good-night to the other woman.

'How are you, child?' he asked, when he joined her.

'Have you heard from Kevin?'

She told him about Kevin's letter. He said that it was a bad time for Kevin's family and it was as well for them they had such a fine son to help them.

'He's a good boy, Sadie.'

'Yes,' said Sadie.

'You must be proud that he's doing his duty by them.'

Walking home she thought about that. She supposed she was proud, she knew he was good, but inside her she couldn't help feeling resentful that his family had to come before her. It's only natural, she told herself, at such a time, and I am just a selfish eejit if I don't understand that! At this rate she was going to end up talking to herself! She called at Lara's.

They were watching a film on television. Sadie sat for a few minutes beside them trying to concentrate and understand what the film was about. A man and woman were quarrelling, shouting at one another as if at any moment they might seize one another by the throat. She did not care if they did. She shifted restlessly on her chair, wishing she could be as peaceful and serene as Lara who never seemed to move and fidget. Sadie scratched her knee, then her left ankle. She noticed Krishna looking down at her ankle as she scratched it. He looked up and their eyes met. He smiled gently, she put her hand back on her lap. Her ankle itched murderously. She just had to scratch it. She tore at it with her fingers, feeling her tights snag under her nails.

'I'll need to be going now, Lara,' she said, half apologetically. She should never have disturbed their peace.

'Come again soon,' said Lara as she showed her out.

'Thanks.'

Sadie went back to her room. The hamburgers were cold and congealed but she was hungry so she sprinkled salt on them and ate them.

'What a life!' she said aloud. 'Nothing but a mad dizzy whirl!'

There was a stampede of feet in the hall and then someone was knocking at her door.

'Can we come in?' asked Rita, already on the way in. She was followed by Sally, Joe and two other boys.

'Hi, honey!' said Joe, stroking his fingers across Sadie's cheek as he passed her.

The boys were carrying brown paper carriers, out of which they lifted cans of beer. They began to take off their coats, Sadie decided she might as well close the door.

'We've come to cheer you up,' said Rita.

'Seeing as you're a grass widow,' said Joe, zipping open the first can.

'I haven't got enough glasses,' said Sadie.

'Don't need glasses,' said Joe, handing her a can. 'What's the matter with the tin?'

Sadie took a can, said, 'Cheers' with the rest and put it to her mouth. Beer trickled down her neck and made her giggle.

'I'd die if I had to sit here on my own of an evening,' said Sally looking round.

'It's not so bad,' said Sadie off-handedly. 'Anyway, Kevin'll be back soon.'

'When's he coming?' asked Rita, who had made herself comfortable on the bed, with a pillow propped behind her head.

'Day or two.' Sadie took another drink.

'Maybe he'll not come back,' said Joe slyly.

'Don't talk daft,' snapped Sadie.

'He's just hoping!' Rita laughed, a big bouncy laugh that came from the middle of her stomach.

Soon they all seemed to be laughing. Sadie could not remember afterwards what it had all been about for no one said anything very amusing. But they were in a mood to laugh and for Sadie it was a relief for she felt as if she had been holding all her laughter up inside her and it had just been waiting to escape. The beer went to her head quickly.

From laughing they went on to singing. Sadie was urged to give them an Irish song.

'Come on, "The Mountains of Mourne"!' cried Rita, waving a tin of beer in the air.

'That's dead corny,' giggled Sadie.

'We like a bit of corn now and then,' said Joe.

'Oh Mary this London's a wonderful sight,' warbled Sadie and then she broke down in giggles.

Mrs Kyrakis had to knock four times before anyone heard her; at least so she told Sadie when they finally opened the door to see her standing there in her dressing gown, her hair in curlers, and her brow creased with irritation.

'This noise have to stop,' she declared, looking into the room. 'No parties here. I cannot sleep for the pandemonium.'

Joe laughed. She took a step into the room and glared at him. Sadie began to apologize, Rita got off the bed to gather up the empty cans. Mrs Kyrakis shook her head.

'This will not happen again,' she declared, stabbing the air with a thick finger. 'Or you are out!'

She went back down the corridor.

'This will not happen again,' said Joe, imitating her accent. 'Or you are out!'

They all started to laugh again.

'You'd better go,' said Sadie. 'I don't want to get thrown into the street.'

'I could come to your rescue,' said Joe, holding out his arms.

'Dead right you could,' said Rita sarcastically. 'Man, you're all heart.'

Joe hung back and let the others go out on the pavement in front of him.

'I don't have to get home yet,' he whispered. 'Me mother allows me to stop up late now I'm big.'

'I don't know why I'm sure.' Sadie tried to close the door but he had his foot well placed.

'Don't you like me, Sadie?'

'You're all right. But you're going now.'

'I don't fancy you being left here all alone.'

'You don't have to worry about me.'

Rita called from the street, 'Are you coming, Joe? We'll miss the tube.'

'You go on,' he called back.

'You're not coming in,' said Sadie.

'Why not?'

'You know why not.'

He shook his head. 'You're a tough 'un. Give me a kiss then before I go.'

She allowed him to kiss her. Afterwards, when he had gone, and she leant against the door, she did not know why. She held the back of her hand against her lips, not understanding herself. She felt unclean. She had been unfaithful to Kevin. Then she told herself not to be so stupid, there was nothing all that wrong in letting another boy kiss her. But of course Kevin would think so, and that was what mattered. She would have to be careful, watch herself.

With the gaiety gone out of it the room looked depressing, rumpled and littered, smelling of beer and tobacco smoke. She opened up the window to let in the night air, wiped up the beer spills, smoothed out the bed. She was tired, wanted to sleep, and not to think any more.

But, once in bed, she could not sleep, and lay with eyes open watching the lights flickering over the ceiling whenever a car passed. She thought about Kevin, imagining him asleep, his dark hair on a pillow in Belfast, with his brothers all around him squashed into a tiny room. And she thought of Joe too, as fair as Kevin was dark, Joe whom she did not like so very much, always pretending to be cynical and so sure of himself, and yet probably underneath he felt as small and uncertain as anyone else. She did not know why she should think about Joe, but she did.

Chapter Eighteen

Mr Kelly came to the house the day after the funeral to offer Kevin his old job back. The scrap business was doing rightly, he said, after a bad spell, he himself was getting no younger, and he could be doing with Kevin's young strong arms.

'I'd take you on as a partner like,' said Mr Kelly. 'We'd split the takings and one day the business'd be yours, lad, for, as you know, I've no son of my own.'

'Is that not a fine offer, Kevin?' cried Mrs McCoy, her face lit with happiness for the first time since her husband had been killed. She turned to Mr Kelly. 'Sure you're a good man, Dan. I've always said so. God look to you. It's the answer to my prayers.'

Mr Kelly twirled his cap round in his fingers. 'Ach, Mary, it's nothing. I'm right fond of Kevin, you know that full well, and I was sorry when I wouldn't have him back before.'

'We needn't go into all that again,' said Mrs McCoy. She filled the kettle, lit the gas with a plop. 'It's all past history and I don't believe in holding old grudges. Isn't that all the cause of the trouble we have around us?

The gas flame hissed under the old kettle. Kevin stared at it, then looked back at his mother and Dan Kelly, who had not even looked at him to ask if he agreed.

'Mr Kelly, I can't do it,' he said.

'Now, Kevin, you're not going to keep an old grudge, are you, son?' said his mother.

'I've no grudge against Mr Kelly.'

'And you enjoyed working in the yard, didn't you? Sure

you used to come back in the evening as contented as anything.'

'I know but –'

He sighed. His mother's tired eyes were fixed on his pleadingly. She wanted him to take the job and bring home the money to help feed the family. They would have to be fed, and Brede did not earn very much as a nursery nurse. Besides, there was the question of Brede's marriage. His mother had never once referred to Kevin's. Brede said that she thought her mother had wiped it out of her mind, that she did not want to believe in it and so she never thought or spoke about it. Whenever Kevin tried to lead up to it she changed the conversation. She did not believe he would return to London either, he was home, and that was that. The years of trouble and their father's death had changed her. It was no wonder, said Brede, they would have to be patient with her.

'Tell Mr Kelly you'll take up his offer, Kevin. You'll get no better one.'

Mr Kelly got up. 'Think it over, boy, and come down and see me at the yard tomorrow.'

'You'll stay for a cup of tea, Dan?' said Mrs McCoy.

'Thanks, Mary, but I'll need to be getting along.'

He left them alone, the mother with her eldest son, her only hope now for any kind of decent life.

'It's a fine chance, son. And one day you'd own the yard. You'd be your own master.'

'But I've been working as a TV mechanic, ma, and going to night school. I like that better.' He was not giving the real reason, he knew it, he could only skirt round it. He did not have it in him to be so brutal to her. She had had enough.

'Well, I don't know as you'd get a job like that here. There's that many shops have got burnt out. And the money'd be better in the yard.'

She made the tea, set the pot near the turned-down flame. He wondered how many times he had watched her go through the same actions. Outside in the back yard the two youngest children were playing with a broken tricycle, fighting over it, crying and squawking every few minutes, but their mother paid no attention. She had heard too many children squawking in her time.

Brede came in, looked from her mother to her brother, feeling the tension between them.

'Kevin's been offered his job back at the yard, Brede. And he's to be Mr Kelly's partner! Isn't that just great?'

'But, ma, Kevin'll have to go back to London,' cried Brede. Mrs McCoy's body stiffened. All colour drained from her face; she looked like an old woman, reminding them of their grandmother in Tyrone.

'We can't expect him to stay here,' went on Brede gently. 'You know we can't.'

'Well, we'll have to see,' said Kevin.

'We haven't enough to live on,' whispered Mrs McCoy. 'We'll starve.'

'We can get help from the National Assistance,' said Brede.

'That it should come to that!' Now Mrs McCoy's voice was bitter. 'I never thought I'd live to see the day, God help us all!'

'There's nothing wrong in getting help from the state,' said Brede. 'Many's a one as had to do it before now. Aunt Patsy's done it for years.'

'I don't want to be likened to your Aunt Patsy. She has no pride in her.'

Mrs McCoy gathered herself up and went through to the front parlour where she slept with the two youngest children. Kevin and Brede looked at one another with misery in their eyes.

'There must be some other way,' said Kevin.

'What?' asked Brede.

'I'm going for a walk. I need to think.'

Kevin walked through the streets till he came to the River Lagan. There he turned off along the towpath where he had often walked with Sadie when they were courting. They had had to meet in secret, afraid that either of their families would see them and try to separate them. But how could he be married in secret, hide a wife in the house? He grinned at the idea of Sadie allowing herself to be hidden anywhere. He felt a tug at his heart: he was missing her. He threw a stone into the river, watching it plop in the middle of the water. And there was his mother, bent and beaten by the hardness of her life, needing him desperately. Needing him even more than Sadie who could survive most disasters. But how could he give up Sadie? She was his wife. He had never felt more confused in his life.

He wandered along the river thinking of Sadie running along the paths to meet him, her long hair flying out in the wind behind her, her cheeks pink and glowing, her eyes bright with mischief and happiness. Life burst out of her like a flower opening in a flood of sunshine. He needed that life. He wished she was here now, so that he could touch her, feel her warmth.

Restlessness would not let him return home and he could not face his mother's eyes. He would go and visit the Hendersons, a young couple they had known and whose children Sadie had looked after. She was Catholic, he was Protestant. They might be able to help him. They were older and had more experience than he.

When he turned into their street he saw a gap where Mr Blake's house had been. It had been burned down when a bomb was thrown through his window, and Mr Blake had died in the fire. Mr Blake had been their friend, his and Sadie's, and that was why he had died. Sickness engulfed Kevin, the memory of it all flooding back. He passed by quickly, reached the Hendersons' gate and went up the path.

A strange woman answered the door.

'Are Mr and Mrs Henderson in?' he asked.

'Oh no,' she said. 'They moved away a few months ago. I believe they went to Scotland.'

So they had gone away, seeking refuge in a place where no one would bother them because of their religion. They had not stayed after all. He wished now that he and Sadie had written to them, kept in touch, but they were poor at writing letters, they often meant to, talked of doing it, but one letter each week to their homes had been all they had managed. Recently Sadie had not even done that for when her mother did write back she wrote to say that Sadie had broken her heart. Kevin walked disconsolately home through the streets.

When he came in he was met by Gerald.

'Ma's been taken to the hospital,' said Gerald. 'Brede's gone with her.'

Kevin ran all the way to the hospital. Brede was sitting in a corridor, her face the colour of an old sheet.

'For God's sake, what's happened?' cried Kevin.

'She's had a thrombosis. A clot in the leg, something like that, the doctor said.' Brede's voice trailed away.

'Will she die?'

'I don't know. She's not been well since her operation. She's had no chance to get over it. And I suppose da's death has brought it on.'

Kevin sat beside Brede, his hands over his face, the possibility of his mother's death on his conscience. Brede told him that he was being silly, it was no fault of his.

'If only I'd said I'd take the job!'

'You couldn't have said it.'

A doctor came shortly to talk to them. Their mother should be all right, she had been lucky but she would be in hospital for a good while and then she ought to go to a convalescent home. She was sleeping now but if they came back tomorrow they could see her.

The next morning Kevin went down to the scrapyard. Mr

Kelly was bent over a pile of junk. He lifted his head when Kevin called out and straightened his back. He was a stocky little man with muscles like steel from years of heavy lifting. Kevin picked his way through the scrap.

'Well, Kevin, have you thought it over?'

Kevin nodded. 'I'd like to come back for a while, Mr Kelly, but I can't promise to stay for ever. If you'll take me on temporary-like. I have a wife in London you know,' he added awkwardly and Mr Kelly nodded. 'But I'll need to stay at home for a while to help my mother.'

'Right, son.' Mr Kelly held out his hand and Kevin took it. 'Glad to have you back for as long as you want. We always got on well, didn't we now?'

It was true, Kevin said. They agreed on his wage and that he would start the next day.

'Will you get your card sent from London?' asked Mr Kelly. 'I'll need to have it stamped.'

Kevin nodded. He had not thought of that. He would have to write a letter of resignation to Mr Davis and explain the situation. He sighed.

'It's not easy for you, boy,' said Mr Kelly. 'I understand. But how could you walk out on your family now?'

'I couldn't,' said Kevin.

As he left the yard Kate Kelly came out of her house. She stopped, startled at seeing him. Long dark hair fell over her shoulders. When he was close to her he realised it was a wig.

'Hello, Kevin.' She put her hand to her face half covering it.

'Hello, Kate.'

'Nice to see you back,' she said.

'I'm sorry about –'

She shrugged, touched the back of her head briefly. 'I've got over it,' she said, but he could see from her eyes that she had not.

'Are you not working then?'

'I'm just stopping at home at the moment helping me mum. Couldn't face going back to work.' Her lip trembled.

'You will, one of these days.'

'Sure.'

'Kate, I believe that Gerald was –'

'Skip it!' Her voice was harsh. 'It's not your fault. You don't have to apologize for him.'

'He's on a bad road.'

'There's plenty like him about.' She hesitated. 'Will you come in and have a cup of tea?'

'All right.'

He went because he was sorry for her. She was pleased to have him sitting in her mother's kitchen. She made a pot of tea and set out a plate of buttered potato bread. The kitchen was clean and bright. The Kellys were never hard up and they were a much smaller family than the McCoys. Kevin found it peaceful in the kitchen with the sun shining on the red lino-leum. The potato bread melted in his mouth. It was like old times, sitting here, talking to Kate, drinking tea, though Kate now looked different. She used to dress herself up, make up her eyes with blue and green spread across the lids and false eyelashes so long that he teased her about them, saying they were so long you could sweep the streets with them.

'You're staring at me as if I'm a right looking sight,' she said.

'You're not. You're as bonny as ever.'

She blushed. 'Ach, sure you've a sweet tongue on you, Kevin McCoy.'

He drank two cups of hot sugary tea and ate several pieces of warm potato bread.

'I baked it myself,' said Kate. 'I've nothing much else to do. Look in any time you fancy for a cup of tea.'

He promised that he would. Gerald was on the other side of the street when he left the Kellys' house.

'Don't tell me you're taking up with that bitch again!' said Gerald.

Kevin seized his shoulder. 'Don't speak like that! You've done enough to her. Too much. And I'm taking up with nobody. I've a wife of my own.'

'Aye, a dirty ould Prod.'

Kevin hit him then, right across the face, and he hit him so hard that he knocked him on to his back on the pavement. Kevin walked home quickly.

'Brede,' he called.

She came down the stairs.

He told her what had happened. 'Brede, I don't know what to do with that boy. I know that knocking him about won't help but God help me I don't know what to do.'

'I don't know either,' said Brede.

That evening Gerald returned home late. Kevin and Brede sat up in the kitchen wondering if he would come home at all, half wishing that he would not but not even admitting it to one another. He is our brother, they told one another, and only fifteen years old, still a child in some ways but with more violence behind him than most middle-aged men. They could not strike him out of their thoughts so easily. Kevin had meant to write to Sadie but his mind was full of so many things, his mother, Gerald, work at the scrapyard, that he could not settle to it. He dreaded telling Sadie that he was taking a temporary job here.

Gerald came in with a bleeding head. He collapsed on a chair in the kitchen, weak with the loss of blood, unable to speak. Brede told him to sit still; she filled a basin with warm water and Kevin went for the doctor.

The doctor asked no questions. He had mopped up too much blood to ask anything any more. To save life was his job, not interrogate patients. 'It'll need a few stitches,' he said. 'Can you hold his head, Kevin?'

Gerald cried out when the stitches were being put in. Kevin held him still; Brede stood by handing the doctor cotton wool and dressings as he required them.

'Well, you'll live, Gerald,' said the doctor. 'If you stay out of trouble, that is. Next time you might not be as lucky.'

Kevin saw the doctor out.

'Terrible way these youngsters are going,' sighed the doctor.

Kevin and Brede helped Gerald up to bed. He was moaning with the pain but the doctor had given him a sedative so that he would sleep. Michael wakened with the noise, lifted himself up on his elbow to ask what was wrong.

'Gerald's had his head split open,' said Kevin. 'And no doubt he deserved it. Don't you ever be as big a fool, Michael.'

The clock on the kitchen dresser showed it was two o'clock. Kevin yawned, weary to the centre of his body. He should have gone to bed early for he had a long day ahead in the scrapyard.

'Perhaps that'll have taught him a lesson,' said Brede.

'Perhaps,' said Kevin, but he did not believe it. If it was as easy as that this country of his would never have had as much trouble as it had.

He would write to Sadie tomorrow, he thought, when he lay down in bed. He slept intermittently, and whenever he woke he heard Gerald moaning in his sleep in the next room.

Chapter Nineteen

'I'm real sorry to be losing Kevin,' said Mr Davis. He wiped his hands on a rag. He had been working on the back of a television set when Sadie came into the shop.

Sadie stared at him over the top of the set. 'Losing him?' she said.

'Yes, I had a letter from him this morning.' Mr Davis nodded at an envelope lying on the shelf. 'Of course I understand.'

Sadie saw from where she stood that the writing on the envelope was indeed Kevin's. She put out her hand and then stopped for of course she could not lift someone else's letter. Something odd was happening to her: it was like being caught up in a dream.

'Are you going back over?' asked Mr Davis.

'Well, no—er, I'm not sure.' She was not sure of anything.

'Are you all right, lass? You look sort of shaken up. I suppose you must be worried about Kevin being over there with all that trouble going on.'

'He's not coming back?' she said, trying not to make it sound too much like a question.

'Not for a while, he says. Course I can't keep his job open for him, you realize that, Sadie. After all, he might be gone for months.'

'Months,' she echoed.

She moved towards the door.

He frowned. 'You did know, didn't you?'

'Yes, yes. Certainly I knew.'

'I'll be sending him his card,' he called after her. 'You can tell him.'

The door chimed when she opened it. The chime stayed in her ears as she ran through the streets. She had not been home yet since coming from work: there might be a letter waiting for her. There must be a letter. One that would explain everything and tell her it was all a big mistake.

There was no letter. She searched twice through the pile on the hall table reading all the names carefully though she could see at a glance that none were for her. Someone might have taken hers by mistake. She rapped on Mrs Kyrakis's door. Mrs Kyrakis opened it, wiping her mouth with a napkin.

'Well,' she said, 'what you want now?'

'You don't know if there was a letter for me today, do you?'

'If there is one it will be in the hall.'

The door closed. Sadie went to every door knocking and asking, 'You haven't taken a letter of mine by mistake, have you?' Blank stares, shrugs, one or two said, 'Sorry, dear.' The woman with the cats asked her to see the cats. The smell in the room was putrid. There were cats but no letters of any kind for the woman seldom received one at all. Sadie went next door.

'He will write soon, I'm sure,' said Lara soothingly. 'And explain it all. He wouldn't just forget you, Sadie.'

'I know,' said Sadie miserably. 'At least I hope he wouldn't. But he's got this awful strong thing about his family and them being Catholics and dozens of them and everything.'

'But you are his wife.'

Lara gave her a cup of coffee. Krishna sat by the table at the window studying, his back turned on the emotions of the two women. He rested his head on one hand, with his other hand he wrote slowly and meticulously.

'I'd better go,' said Sadie. 'I don't want to disturb you.'

'You are not disturbing us,' said Lara.

'What can I do?' wailed Sadie. 'He's so far away.'

Krishna looked round. 'You could send a telegram.'

Sadie worded it with his help. 'WORRIED BY YOUR LETTER TO MR DAVIS. LOVE SADIE.' She hurried off to the post office and once the message was sent, felt a little better. She went to Rita's and could not stop herself telling her. From the look on Rita's face she knew that Rita thought he would not come back at all.

'Easy come, easy go these days,' said Rita. 'Nothing lasts for ever.'

Sadie scarcely slept all night. She got up from time to time to look at the clock, wishing that morning would come. When it did she rose, dressed and sat by the window waiting for the telegraph boy. She did not go to work till he came bringing the little yellow envelope. She met him on the doorstep.

'MOTHER IN HOSPITAL,' she read. 'LETTER FOLLOWS. LOVE KEVIN.'

She went into Lara's room and read it to her.

'So there is a very reasonable explanation,' said Lara. 'I told you that there would be. You must be patient now and wait for his letter and then you will know more.'

Sadie arrived at work an hour late.

'And just where have you been?' demanded Miss Cullen.

'My mother-in-law's very ill,' said Sadie. 'I was waiting for a telegram from my husband.'

Miss Cullen sniffed. She found it difficult to believe in Sadie's husband. The girl looked far too young to be married at all. 'Don't let it happen again,' she said.

Sadie said nothing, caring not at all if the woman would sack her for then she could leave London and take the train to Liverpool and get on the boat and go home and see what Kevin was doing. Her mind stopped racing for she couldn't see herself walking up Kevin's street opening the door and calling out, 'It's Sadie.'

'Cheer up, ducks,' said Rita. 'There's plenty more fish in

the sea. We're going to a party tonight. What about coming with us?'

Sadie went to the party and danced all evening with Joe. But before anyone knew she slipped away, wanting suddenly to be home, even though it was to be by herself.

Three days later Kevin's letter came. So he had gone back to work in the scrapyard! Sadie bit her lip, jealous already that Kate Kelly would be seeing him. But Kate would not take him away from her, she had not been able to before. Yes, but things were different now. He said that he did not know how long he would have to stay but he would come back as soon as he could. He wanted to come, he missed her, but he could not leave his family in such a mess.

'He's right, you know, Sadie,' said Father Mulcahy, who called later in the evening. 'Just think, his mother in hospital, seven children not working.'

'It's ridiculous to have all those children,' Sadie burst out. 'Yes, it is. His mother never should have had them. It's wicked that your church should encourage them. Wicked!'

She burst into tears. The priest comforted her and sighed and said that it was all a great pity, he did not himself think it was good to bring big families into the world, but she must remember that Mrs McCoy would not regret having a single one of her children.

'Now that she's got them,' said Sadie. 'But if she'd never had them she wouldn't have missed them.'

'The church will change in time, I'm sure, Sadie.'

'When enough people have suffered!'

She felt bitter that night and lonely. She wrote a long letter to Kevin blaming everything on his religion, telling him it was stupid and wicked and brought nothing but trouble. She licked the flap of the envelope, stuck on the stamp defiantly and went out through the late night streets to post it before she would change her mind. It was a wild letter but she did not care. Kevin needed to be jolted, to be reminded that she was not going to sit and wait like a cabbage till it came into his head to return.

The letter was on her mind as soon as she awoke. Her stomach moved queasily. Had she said too much? It was one of her faults, launching out with all guns firing and then later regretting it. As she washed and dressed she thought of Kevin opening the letter, getting angrier and angrier, and she would not even be there to say, 'I didn't mean it just as badly as that!'

She pulled on her coat and ran. It was early yet, the street lights still shone in the dawn light. The box might not have been cleared. It mustn't have been cleared!

A pain caught her in the ribs as she reached the pillar box. She gasped, rubbing her chest. She took the last step to the box and her eye jumped at once to the little white slot announcing the next collection. No. 2! The first lift was 7.15. She looked at her watch. Twenty past seven. She had just missed it. And her letter was away on its journey to Kevin beyond her reach.

She leant against the cold red pillar box. It was a rainy morning. A splatter of rain hit her face. A milkman swinging a crate of bottles stopped and asked if she was all right.

'Yes,' she said sluggishly.

She heaved herself off the box and wandered back to her room. She sat on the unmade bed. If she had enough money she would go to Ireland and see him. But then she knew she could borrow some from Rita, even hitch-hike to Liverpool. That was not the reason she was not going. It was not right to go, to follow him when she could do nothing. She would have to stay with her mother and her mother would say, 'I told you so, Sadie Jackson! You always were one to act too fast. Act first and think later, that's been your motto. Now look where it's got you!'

Rain flailed the window panes. She got up and closed the curtains. The world did not appeal to her this morning and she was certainly in no mood to sell elastic. She took off her skirt and shoes and crawled back into the soft warm bed.

She slept all day, wakened as the street was darkening again. She wakened to the sound of someone knocking on her door. She put her old dressing gown around her to open it.

'Hi!' said Joe.

'You!' she said.

'That's not a very sweet greeting.'

'I don't feel sweet today.'

'Rita said you'd not been at work. I was worried in case you were ill and here all alone.'

She pushed back her hair. 'I've been sleeping all day. I must be an awful looking sight.'

'You're as beautiful as ever.'

'Oh you!'

'Are you asking me in then?'

'I suppose you might as well come in now you're here.'

She told him all her troubles, about Kevin and his large, demanding, needy family, about his religion and hers, about the strong letter she had written. Joe listened quietly to the great flood of words that poured out of her. She had never really talked so fully to anyone about Kevin, not even Lara. Lara did not want to know too much.

'I'm sorry, Sadie,' said Joe. 'What a scene!'

'What a scene,' she echoed gloomily.

'I'm sorry,' he said. 'Honest I am.'

'Thanks.'

'Are you hungry?'

She found that she was. Joe went off to buy fish and chips. She dressed, made the bed, tidied the room, glad that another human being was coming back into it, that she would have someone to eat and talk with. She had always needed company, had never before sat around in rooms alone doing nothing.

Fish and chips and Coca Cola. She and Kevin had often had the same for their supper. She put the thought of Kevin out of her mind.

'Fancy going to the pictures?' Joe asked, when they had finished eating.

Yes, she did fancy it very much, she decided. It was a long time since she had been to the cinema; usually Kevin was studying or playing darts or they had no money.

They enjoyed the film and afterwards Joe brought her home, parting with her after only a quick kiss on her cheek. She felt grateful to him for that.

'Thanks, Joe,' she called after him. 'For the movie and everything.'

'Joe's a good friend,' she told Rita next morning.

Rita rolled her eyes. 'Is he growing on you?'

'Don't talk daft!'

Miss Cullen heaved into sight so Rita disappeared. Where had Sadie been the previous day? Miss Cullen wished to know. She might at least have sent some word to say she was ill.

'I wasn't ill,' said Sadie, the devil rising in her, wanting to enjoy the astonishment on the other woman's face.

'You weren't ill? Why weren't you at work then?'

'I just didn't fancy coming.'

Sadie was given her cards more or less on the spot. She sailed happily into the cloakroom to tell the girls.

'I've been fired,' she cried, and waved an envelope. 'One week's wages.' Less what she owed for a dress. But she did not mention that. That would reduce the drama of it.

They clustered around, half envious, half pitying her.

'There are other jobs,' she said gaily. 'Doesn't do to get in a rut.'

She had always hated staying too long in one job: she was bored before long. Her mother used to despair, holding her rollered head between her hands and moaning, 'You'll be the death of me yet, Sadie Jackson!'

When she emerged into the street she wanted to run and jump and sing. She was free! And inside that big ugly building the girls were shifting from foot to foot selling shoes and cards and elastic and yawning and wishing the clock hands would crawl round and release them for their coffee break and then lunch and then finally to go home. That was no way to spend a life.

Sadie idled round the shop windows choosing clothes, bright kitchen ware, curtains. She was not going back to that grisly lonely room for her first day of freedom. She wandered until she came to the café where Rita and her friends often gathered. She sat at a table by the window and drank coffee.

She had had a feeling Joe would come.

'Surprised?' she asked, when he came in through the doorway and saw her. 'I've been fired!'

He laughed. 'You don't seem bothered.'

'I'm not. That stupid Cullen woman was driving me round the twist. Oh, I'll go and look for another job tomorrow but today I'm free.'

He knew how to spend a day of freedom; she had thought that he would. He took her to Brighton on the train. He had money which he spent on her, spoiling her, making her laugh and shout in the face of the winter wind. He bought her a yellow silk scarf to tie round her hair, perfume to dab on her wrists, chocolates to eat as they walked along the promenade looking at the green-grey sea. They had lunch in a warm restaurant with soft carpets, served by a waiter with a white napkin over his arm. She did not ask Joe where his money came from. Rita said that he worked hard for spells, earned a lot, then took time off. Sadie did not even want to know how or where he earned his money. It was a day away from the depressing business of trying to make money stretch when obviously it wasn't going to, of talking of what they would do when they were rich. It was good to have a day in which you didn't feel poor.

Chapter Twenty

Kevin tore Sadie's letter into tiny shreds, took it into the yard and stowed it carefully away in the dustbin so that no one else in his family would read even a part of it. Silly little fool! He stood in the yard burning with rage. What was the point in ranting at his mother for having nine children? They were here, weren't they? And the things Sadie had said about his church ... He shook his head, sighed, went back into the kitchen to pick up his plastic lunch box which Brede had filled.

'What were you doing out there?' she asked.

'Nothing.'

'What did Sadie have to say?'

'Nothing.'

'She must be missing you.'

He shrugged. 'I'll be off then, Brede,' he said. He saw the anxious look in her eyes as she watched him go.

As he went through the hall he called up the stairs to the other children, 'Get up and help your sister. And don't be late for school.'

It was like old times going down the street in the early morning with his lunch box in his pocket. Mrs Rafferty was at her door in curlers and apron leaning against the jamb, her sharp eyes missing nothing.

'You back for good then, Kevin, are you?' she called across to him.

'Don't know yet.' He did not slow his stride. He felt her eyes on his back until he turned the corner.

He liked going round the streets in the truck. He liked being on the move, going from district to district, looking at the houses, thinking about the people who lived in them. And Dan Kelly was easy to be with, talkative at times, quiet at others. He was quieter now than he used to be, perhaps because of age, more likely because of the troubled times and of Kate. Many people had things to be quiet about.

'Aye, she's a different girl, Kevin,' he sighed. 'She never goes out. Maybe you could look in and see her now and then. She was always fond of you. Just as a friend, I mean,' he added hastily.

The days passed quickly. They piled scrap on the truck – there was no shortage of that in Belfast – brought it back to the yard, sorted it and shifted it, sold what they could. Kevin looked in on Kate for a few minutes after work every night; she gave him a cup of tea and fresh baked potato or soda scones. After that he went home to find Brede labouring over the cooker, the children clamouring and hungry, Gerald sullen in a corner with few words for Kevin. He hates me, Kevin thought, appalled by the knowledge, not understanding properly how such hate had risen up. He talked a lot to Michael and the next boy Joseph, trying to instil in them that they must not follow Gerald just because he was older, that they had to make up their own minds about things. Kevin felt as if he had aged ten years since his father died.

Their mother's health picked up steadily. They visited her in the evenings, he and Brede, taking one of the other children in turn. She sat up in bed smiling, pleased to see them and hear that all was well. She questioned Brede closely about the housekeeping even though she had complete faith in her. But she had to ask her about everything, the price Brede was paying for butter, were the children going to bed on time, had Joseph been taking his medicine? Brede answered patiently, knowing her mother's ways. And before they left Mrs McCoy would give them instructions, telling them what they already knew. Rent, insurance, milkman. She had to rest easy in her mind.

'You're a good girl, Brede,' she said. 'And you've turned into a fine man, Kevin. It's good to have you back.'

His mother's words stayed in his ears, but in Sadie's voice, ringing like a reproach. When they got home he went into the front parlour where the two youngest children were sleeping, took out the pad of blue lined paper and sat down with the light shaded to write to Sadie. "Dear Sadie," he wrote, then paused to bite the end of the pen. He hated writing letters. He wanted to see her and talk to her. There was an ache in his throat that threatened to choke him. "I am sorry I have not written before but I was mad at your letter. But now I have forgiven you. Mother is getting better but it will take time. I hope to come back soon. Love Kevin." It didn't say enough but he could not think what else to write. He couldn't be bothered to write about Gerald and Michael and Joseph or the scrapyard. And she would certainly not want to hear about Kate.

He went out to post it. As he passed the Raffertys' house Brian came out. Kevin had heard he had been released, and no charge brought. They had been both friends and enemies. Kevin did not stop but Brian called after him, 'Hey, hang on a minute, Kevin.'

Brian fell into step beside him. 'No hard feelings, eh, Kev? Might as well let old scores lie.'

'I suppose,' said Kevin, not caring about the old scores, but not wanting to take up his friendship with Brian Rafferty again.

'I'm glad you saw the light and left that Prod over there in London where she belongs.'

So that was what they thought, that he had left Sadie. He did not answer though part of him wanted to speak out and lay his full claim to Sadie and tell the world he was going back to her. The other part made him keep quiet, to protect his family.

Thinking of his family led to thinking of Sadie's, particularly of her brother Tommy, whom he knew and liked. He wanted to see Tommy, to talk to him of Sadie; he needed to talk to someone about her, to make him feel closer to her.

The streets were fairly quiet for not many people moved about at nights if they could avoid it, unless they had ulterior motives. Some men still went to pubs in spite of the bombings, refusing to give in totally to the disruptors. He might find Tommy in a pub near his home.

There was a risk going to Sadie's home area, that he was aware of, but he had taken it before and he knew his way around. Outside the pub on the corner of the Jacksons' street he paused to look about, then quietly pushed open the door a few inches. The pub was busy, full of noise and smoke. His eyes scanned the men searching for Tommy or Mr Jackson. If the latter was there he would let the door swing back and walk away.

'Are you going in or out then?' asked a man behind him.

He went in, it seemed the easiest thing to do. The man followed him. Kevin frowned, thinking that the man seemed familiar, not wanting to find anyone familiar here but Tommy. And then he saw Tommy leaning against the counter talking to two other men. At the same moment Tommy saw him. He almost called out in surprise but stopped himself in time. He stood staring at Kevin until his friends also turned to look. Tommy put his beer down on the counter and elbowed his way through the crowd.

'Kevin! It is you, isn't it?'

'It's me right enough.'

'Where's Sadie?'

'London.'

The man who had followed Kevin into the pub had now

turned to look at Kevin as well and was eyeing him in a puzzled way as if he should know him.

'Who's that over there?' muttered Kevin.

'Mr Mullet. A friend of me da's. You once had an argument with him when you took Sadie to Bangor. Let's get out of here.'

They left at once, walking quickly, knowing that if Mr Mullet's memory returned they could be followed by a dozen members of the Loyal Orange Lodge who would have gladly flattened Kevin. They walked towards the centre of the city where they went into a café. Sitting in a corner they drank coffee and Kevin told Tommy about Sadie and the death of his father.

'Aye, it's terrible,' sighed Tommy. 'I'm thinking of emigrating myself. I have it in my mind to go to Australia. Sure you'd need to be nuts to want to stay here.'

'Your mother and father'll not like that?'

'Maybe not. With Sadie gone and all. But what can I do? I've my own life to think of. I want to be sure of having one. I can't let them stop me.'

No, agreed Kevin, Tommy could not. For himself it was not so simple. Mr and Mrs Jackson had one another and no young children to support.

'You'll take good care of Sadie, won't you?' said Tommy awkwardly before they parted. 'I'd like to think she was all right.'

'I'll take care of her,' promised Kevin.

Robert, Brede's fiancé, came up from Tyrone for the weekend. He was a pleasant boy with an open face and eyes that followed Brede everywhere.

'He's real soft on you, Brede,' said Kevin, making Brede's cheeks turn pink. 'And he's a nice lad. He'll make you a good husband, I'm thinking.' He was Catholic too so they would have no problems that way. Not that Brede would have thought of marrying a Protestant. It would cause too much trouble, she would say if she was asked; besides, she would like it better to live with someone of her own faith and then they could rear their children together with the same beliefs.

'I don't know when I'll be able to marry him though,' said Brede. 'I've told him so and he wasn't happy.'

'You'll marry him when you're good and ready,' declared Kevin, who saw in his mind Brede going off to Tyrone and himself trapped here unable ever to abandon his mother.

Robert came back the next week-end unexpectedly. 'I've news for you,' he said as he came in through the door, cutting off Brede's cry of surprise. 'I think I know what to do. About your mother and that.'

'Sit down, Robert,' said Kevin. 'And make him a cup of tea, Brede. The man's got a plan in his head.'

Brede filled the kettle, her eyes shining. She trusted Robert, had known he would think of something. He had said that he would before he left the week-end before.

'Well,' said Robert, 'the cottage I have is one of three joined together.'

'They're on the farm,' Brede interrupted, 'and when you look out of the window all you can see is fields and sheep and trees.'

'Now,' said Robert, 'the other two happen to be empty.'

'Ah!' said Kevin, leaning back in his chair.

Brede set two cups of tea on the table. 'You'll be hungry, I'm thinking?' she said to Robert.

'I could eat a bite,' he said. 'My mother and father live in a cottage on its own a few yards over,' he explained to Kevin. 'My dad's been on this farm for twenty years. Mr O'Brien, the farmer, is short of workers and that's why the two cottages are standing empty.'

'So he'd rent them to us?' said Kevin slowly. 'A family this size'd certainly need two. You couldn't get seven kids in one.'

Robert looked up at Brede first before he answered. 'Aye well, he wouldn't rent them exactly. He'll only have farm workers in them, you see. But he'd let you have them if you were to work for him, Kevin.'

'Work for him? On the farm you mean?'

'You wouldn't mind that so much, would you, Kevin?' said Brede eagerly. 'After all, you'd be out in the air all day and we'd be away from these dirty streets. You'd work with animals and crops instead of old scrap and smashed motor cars. Wouldn't you like that better? It's beautiful there, in County Tyrone.'

It might have been heaven, from the softness in her voice and the happiness in her face, the way she talked of it. Robert looked at her fondly and Kevin felt a rush of homesickness for Sadie. He left the table abruptly to go and stand by the window. Brede flipped over Robert's bacon in the pan and dropped in an egg.

'Great smell, Brede,' said Robert.

She put the bacon and egg on a plate and set it in front of him. 'Now eat that and you'll feel the better for it.' She rested her hands on her hips. 'What do you think then, Kev?'

He turned to her. 'Wouldn't it be fine for all of us to get away from here? It'd be better too for Gerald.'

'He could get in trouble just as easy in County Tyrone. There's trouble enough near the border. And Provos too.'

'But not as many. And he might change when he gets out into the country. It's a chance.' Her voice had changed now: it was pleading. 'And ma would love it, to go back to the place where she grew up. She's never been happy in the city. She's missed the flowers and trees –'

'All right, don't go on!' cried Kevin fiercely.

Robert stopped eating. He looked in surprise at Kevin, fork half way to his mouth. Brede's lower lip moved, then her top teeth came down and held it fast.

'I'm sorry,' said Kevin. 'I didn't mean to shout. But you seem to have forgotten one thing, Brede. Sadie! Even you don't want to know about her now.'

'That's not true,' whispered Brede.

'I have a wife in England, Robert. My family wishes she didn't exist but she does and I can't just leave her. I don't want to. You'll know how I feel even though you're not married yet to Brede.'

Robert looked uncomfortable. 'Aye,' he sighed. 'I know.'

'But I'm not asking you to leave her,' said Brede. 'She could come to Tyrone with us!' Her face lit up again. 'The two of you could live in one cottage with two of the children, Robert and I could have another two, and ma would have three with her. We can all help one another.'

'Like they do in Israel,' said Robert.

'You don't mind, Robert,' said Kevin 'starting your married life with Brede's family running all over you?'

'No,' he said, for he knew that it was only that way that he would have Brede at all. And he wanted Brede, he was sure of that, for being with her was like a long sunny day that went on and on.

'Go on, finish your tea, Robert,' said Brede. 'I don't like the sight of a hungry man. We'll manage with the money, Kev, for ma'll have her widow's pension and the family allowances. And maybe Sadie and I can get jobs on the farm too. I wouldn't mind working in the house cleaning and mending.'

'Sadie might mind,' said Kevin bluntly. 'Have you thought of that?'

'Surely not,' said Brede. 'Once she sees it's the only way.'

'I don't think I could ask her to do all that for me. Have two children to live with us, work for my family, live in the middle of County Tyrone.' The more he pictured it the less he saw Sadie there, swamped by McCoys, partaking in their commune. 'It's a lot to ask of anyone.'

'But she's your wife,' Brede objected. 'Surely when you're married you expect to help one another out?'

'Help yes, but sacrificing yourself altogether? That's a different matter.'

'But Robert's doing it for me.'

'Ay well ... that's different. After all, he lives in Tyrone already, it's his home.'

'Does Sadie like London all that much?' asked Brede.

'No,' said Kevin, and then he could stand no more of it. For the first time he could not talk with his sister Brede. She seemed not to understand. To her it was a simple thing, the answer to her prayers. She saw them all living in three cottages as happy as sandboys, with the birds singing overhead, not a ripple to disturb the peace. And yet she knew Sadie. He opened the kitchen door, saying that he was going for a walk.

'Will you think it over?' she said. 'Please!'

He would think it over, he gave her his promise before he went out. The streets were the only place he could be alone to think and not be badgered by his family. He walked, with his hands bunched into the pockets of his jacket for warmth, his collar up against the whip of the wind. There was a disturbance further along past the scrapyard; instinctively he turned about taking another way. He headed for the river for there he could find peace.

The water was dark, lapping gently, soothing his brain. He leant against a tree, watching the dark shadows, listening to the sound of the night. In many ways he would not mind living in the country: all the things that Brede said about it were true. It was something that he would not be afraid to try even though he liked the town with streets, people, shops, and always something going on. He would be prepared to try it but every time he reached that point he could go no further. For there was Sadie barring the way. How could Sadie live next door to his mother? His mother was a peaceful woman but he sensed that she and Sadie would not hit it off: there was too much that was different between them. How could Sadie take seven children and a sister and brother-in-law? And all Catholics?

He could hear her voice.

'Set up in a commune with eleven Micks? You've got to be joking!'

Chapter Twenty-one

A letter from Kevin. Sadie stood in the hall and looked at it, not rushing back into her room as she would once have done to see what was in it. Every letter he wrote, the few that there had been, had annoyed her in some way or other. In one he had said that he had forgiven her. That had made her rage! She did not want his forgiveness and thought he had a queer cheek on him for thinking he was holy enough to grant it. 'Who do you think you are?' she had written back. 'A priest?' She had told Rita who had shaken her head and said it was time Sadie was forgetting him altogether for there was Joe just crazy about her, ready to give her anything. Sadie did not answer Rita. How could she forget Kevin? Sure, he annoyed her, but when she thought of his dark eyes and the way he had of looking at her she melted right to the middle.

Mrs Kyrakis shuffled along the passage to see if there was any mail for her.

'One minute,' she called, when she saw Sadie hovering in the hall. 'I tell you before.' She waved her fat finger. 'Now I tell you the last time. No more parties in your room. The noise last night is enormous.'

The noise from many rooms in the house was enormous but Sadie did not dare say so. The West Indians sang and played their gramophone so that you could hear it plainly a block away. Sadie thought Mrs Kyrakis was determined to get her out. She probably wanted the room for a relative, Rita had suggested.

Sadie took the letter into her room. She opened it. It was

the longest letter he had ever written. She separated the pages in her hands, then began to read quickly.

He told her that his family was considering a move to Tyrone. His mother, who was now out of hospital, was desperate to go back and leave the streets of Belfast behind her. Kevin went on to tell Sadie of their plan, that she should come and live with them too. He said that at first he had thought it wasn't on, but after a while he realised there was nothing else on. The family couldn't get the house without him and if they stayed in Belfast he would have to stay too. Sadie couldn't come to live with him in this street, so wouldn't it be better to at least try it in Tyrone?

'You've got to be jokin'!' she said aloud, in horror, thinking of all those McCoys, all Catholics, with their crosses and holy pictures on the walls trooping off to mass every Sunday, and the priest calling and saying, 'It can't be easy for you being the odd one out.'

'Kevin McCoy, your head's cut!' She read the letter again, to make sure she had got the message right. But she had. He was asking her to come and live with his whole family and work for them! She wondered what he would have said if she'd asked him to live with her ma with her pictures of the Royal Family on the wall and a mural of King Billy on his white horse painted on the gable end of the house.

She would be late for work! She pushed the letter into her bag, reached for her coat. Outside she met Krishna.

'Good morning, Sadie.' He was never in a hurry, left always in good time to go to work.

But even though she was late she could not resist stopping to tell him about Kevin's letter.

'But that is good,' said Krishna. 'It is better when families can all be together.'

'But not his family and me,' said Sadie. 'I'd be outnumbered.'

'Or you could become one of them. That would be even better.'

'You've got to be joking,' she muttered to herself as she hurried along to the supermarket where she had a temporary job. Everything was temporary at the moment. She worked at a cash point sitting beside a till ringing up the purchases. It was hard work heaving all the groceries around, bags of potatoes, tins of beans and fruit, cartons of soap powder, and especially at the week-end when the store was jammed with people pushing and complaining. By the evening her arms and shoulders ached and her neck felt stiff when she bent it. But she had to eat. Joe was working too, as a labourer, working long hours, making big money. On Sundays they went out and spent it.

That evening Rita and Sally came with Joe. They sat around talking, marvelling over the idea of Sadie going to live in the backwoods of Tyrone.

'London's the place for you, Sadie love,' said Joe.

They were talking quietly but before long Mrs Kyrakis arrived at the door to announce that she had put up long enough with the noise next door to her room. Sadie would have to leave at the end of the week! Mrs Kyrakis shuffled back to her own room.

'If you own a house in London you can behave like God,' said Sadie.

'She's probably got sixty-five cousins due to fly in from Cyprus,' said Joe.

'You can move in with us, Sadie,' said Rita. 'Can't she, Sally?'

'Sure. We can squash up.'

'Thanks,' said Sadie. 'It'll just be temporary of course. Until I find my own room.'

'You don't have to do that,' said Rita.

'But Kevin and I need a room of our own,' said Sadie, and then saw that they were looking at her.

'But he's not coming back, is he?' said Sally.

'I suppose not,' said Sadie wearily. It did not seem possible, that he wouldn't. 'Can I come and stay till I know what I'm doing?'

As long as she wanted, they said, and Joe looked pleased. He winked at Sadie but she did not wink back. She wanted to go and sit in a corner and howl, like she'd done as a small child when hurt and bewildered.

At the end of the week she packed up their things, hers and Kevin's, the few possessions which they had collected during their marriage, the coloured mugs, plates, cushion covers. She was thinking about her marriage as if it was over and yet she could not believe that. She loved him, they had fought for one another, gone through all sorts of terrible times, even left their families. To be beaten now! She wrote him a letter trying to tell him what she felt, saying that she loved him and wanted to live with him but she didn't know how she could go to Tyrone with his family. It took her a long time, trying to put the words down properly so that he would not read it the wrong way. She told him too that she was moving in with Rita for Mrs Kyrakis wanted their room. She put the new address at the bottom and said that she hoped to hear from him soon.

It was sad to leave the room, the first place they had lived together. In the beginning how she had hated it, wanted to get away, had called it a prison!

'Now then, don't be such an eejit,' she said to herself. 'Sure it's only a room. There'll be others.'

She shared Rita's room, sleeping on a divan bed, which in the day-time they used as a settee. Clothes, clean, wet, and dirty, draped the room constantly. Rubbish gathered in corners. Hairs clogged the bathroom sink. Dishes lay unwashed on the draining board until Sadie set to and did the lot. Some days she felt that she couldn't stand the mess any more, then she put on her old jeans and washed and scrubbed the flat from end to end. She was supposed to be untidy, her mother had told her so all her life. But this was squalor! She grinned at herself. She was beginning to think like a prig!

'My, you're the real domesticated one,' yawned Rita, who hated anything to do with domesticity and wished that she could live off paper plates and cups and throw everything away.

But they were kind to her, and they were good-natured. No one ever fought, and from what Sadie had heard about girls in other flats, that at least was something. Rita and Sally were full of tales of girls fighting over boyfriends and dishes and who should clean the bath. Sally and Rita would never fight over cleaning the bath, thought Sadie, for neither of them would ever ever think of doing it.

Sadie did not mind picking their hairs from the sink or washing the dishes but she did mind sharing Rita's room for she never seemed to be on her own. Other people sat in it till late every evening and afterwards she and Rita lay down in a fug of cigarette smoke. Then Rita would start to chatter, raking over the gossip of their crowd, just when Sadie wanted to close her eyes and think of Kevin, and with him in her mind drift into sleep. This was only temporary of course, she told herself every night and morning, otherwise she could not put up with it. She was only waiting until Kevin came to take her away.

'Have patience,' Lara told her, when she went to visit her after work one day.

'I can't always have patience,' said Sadie a little irritably. 'I'm not a very patient person. I think I'm doing very well.'

Lara laughed. 'Yes, you are doing very well.'

Sadie took the baby and bounced him on her knee. He laughed at her, ducking his head against her cheek. She swung him up high so that he laughed even more.

'I'd like to have a baby one day, Lara.'

'I expect you will,' Lara put out her arms. 'Come now, time for food. Stay and eat with us, Sadie. Would you like to?'

Sadie enjoyed Lara's curry. It was pleasing to sit at the table with Lara and Krishna and eat well-cooked food. Usually they ate frozen food heated up in the flat, unless Sadie made the effort to cook a proper meal. It was nice to be away from the flat for a while, and from Rita and Sally too.

When she left Lara and Krishna, she called on Mr Dooley and his dog. They were so pleased to see her that she vowed to call more often, spend fewer evenings sitting in the flat or the café with a crowd of people that bored her most of the time. It was a way of living she had drifted into.

'The street is not the same, Sadie, without you here,' said Mr Dooley.

'I wasn't here all that long.'

'Long enough.'

She wished she was back, in the dingy room, with Kevin. She sighed. Life had taken a wrong turn somewhere.

'When is Kevin returning?' asked Mr Dooley. 'He has been gone a long time.'

'Sometime,' said Sadie.

The winter was moving on; soon it would be spring. The evenings were lengthening and making Sadie restless.

She met Father Mulcahy in the street and told him about Tyrone. She had known what he would say to her but as she listened she wondered if he could be right. Was she being stubborn? Should she go and do her duty by Kevin's family as he said?

'You took him for richer, for poorer, for better, for worse.'

'But it wouldn't work,' she cried. 'It would be crazy.'

'You must search your heart, Sadie,' he told her.

She had searched it so often that she no longer knew what she really felt. She argued constantly with herself, sometimes thinking she should go and make the best of it, but most times deciding that she could not, knowing that there was too much stacked against her to take the road to Tyrone. She might end up by hating Kevin and all the McCoys put together.

Chapter Twenty-two

Kevin got off the bus and waited by the side of the road until it had turned the corner. Then he looked around, at the green fields and hedges, at the trees which were still bare but promised to bud at any moment. He took in a lungful of the sharp clean air. It was quiet, so quiet that he was aware of every sound, a distant tractor, a bird cheeping, the small sigh of wind through the trees.

He walked close to the hedge letting his fingers trail against it, feeling the dampness that remained of the morning dew. A horse was grazing in the field, greyish-white, with the heavy legs of a farm horse. He looked up briefly at Kevin, tossed his head, then returned to the fat grass.

The farmhouse was large and square, red-bricked, a solid house that suggested peace and quiet and security. It might be false security, no one could be sure, for there was no real peace anywhere in the province. Gunmen visited lonely farmhouses from time to time looking to put a bullet through the farmer's head. Red creeper climbed the walls of the house, a large copper beech stood in the middle of the lawn in front of it. Close by the barns were grouped. Kevin liked the look of the barns; he could live in one of those, he thought, and smiled. He liked the look of the whole scene.

After half a mile farther on he came to the farm cottages. On the left stood one on its own; on the right a group of three, terraced. They were small but gave out a feeling of being cared for, with the window frames freshly painted, and trees protecting them from the wind. Yellow curtains hung at the windows of the first cottage; the windows of the other two were blank. He peered through, saw empty, rather small rooms. But he was not used to large rooms so that did not bother him. There were other things that did.

The thought of Sadie living in a flat with Rita and Sally bothered him. He hadn't liked them very much with their silly giggles and fluttery eyes, their way of looking round the room as if they'd never seen anything as cheap and nasty before. He had always thought of Sadie in their own room keeping his place for him, until he went back. But then he had not gone back. And he could not blame her, Mrs Kyrakis had wanted the room, she had to live somewhere, the girls had offered their flat. She would be sitting with them in the evenings giggling and gossiping and boys would be coming in and out. Joe would be coming in and out. That bothered him.

He tried instead to think of Sadie living in one of the cottages, coming out through the door to hang up her washing and meeting his mother coming to hang up hers. The picture did not gel. He saw her more easily sitting in Rita's flat with Joe eyeing her, making her laugh.

'Kevin!'

He turned to see Robert coming along the path. He wore corduroy trousers and a sweater, and there was mud on his boots. He was smiling.

'Grand to see you. Come on and meet my mother and father.'

He took Kevin to their cottage. Mr and Mrs Burke were kind and friendly. They had spent a lifetime in the country, could speak only of the farm, thought the town was a place for the idle and the wicked. It would be good for Kevin's family to get away from it all, they said, and Kevin agreed. They would welcome the McCoys and do everything they could to make them feel at home. Kevin thanked them. He could see his mother and Robert's getting along nicely, having cups of tea together and chatting about the children and the terrible state of the world. His mother would not stray far from the farm once she got here: it would be a retreat for her. There was nothing wrong with that, Kevin decided, not for her, but he could not see Sadie in retreat, nor himself either.

He had lunch with the Burkes. The meal was a big plateful of Irish stew followed by steamed jam pudding.

'Boy, that was great!' he said. The food sat well in his stomach.

'I like to see a man eat a good meal,' said Robert's mother contentedly.

'I'm sure our Brede will look after Robert well.'

'We've no doubts on that, Kevin. We're right fond of the girl already.' Robert smiled. Everything was going to be all right. Kevin could see Brede here, smiling too. She would be contented, probably grow in the end like Robert's mother, a pink-cheeked country-woman whose life centred around her kitchen and garden, taking pleasure in seeing the menfolk come in from a hard day outside to sit at the table and do justice to her cooking. But he could not see Sadie in such a rôle.

After lunch Robert took Kevin to meet Mr O'Brien the farmer. He gave Kevin a firm handshake. He was a big man who looked as if he lived in the open air. Red cheeks with small purple veins, clear eyes. They all seemed so healthy, thought Kevin, and unfussed. In their street in Belfast the women were shrill and harped at their children, the men were dark-faced and wary. There was reason for them to be that way: they had had plenty to set their nerves on edge and it was a miracle that they had stayed as sane as they had.

'I'll leave you then,' said Robert, 'and get back to my work. See you later, Kevin.'

'Shall we take a walk round?' Mr O'Brien suggested to Kevin. 'I'll show you the barns to begin with.'

'They're fine looking barns,' said Kevin, as they turned their feet towards them. 'Sure they're a nice square shape.'

'They are,' said Mr O'Brien, who was proud of his barns,

his home, and his farm. 'Do you like the country, Kevin?'

'Oh yes.'

'You look a strong lad to me. I could make good use of those arms.'

'I've done a lot of heavy work in my time.' He had wanted to do different work, take apart television sets and radios, understand how they worked. But it wasn't easy to do what you wanted in this world. There were many men who would be glad of a job at all.

The barns smelled of hay and animals. The children would love it here, with hay to roll in, animals to help with, fields to run free in. They needed the chance of it. Kevin sighed and Mr O'Brien raised an eyebrow.

'Anything wrong, lad?'

Kevin shook his head.

Mr O'Brien conducted him round the farm showing him every field, every animal. They saw most of it from his Land-Rover. Mr O'Brien said that he hoped Kevin would get his driving licence for he would often have to drive.

'There's plenty of variety in the work, you know. Not like standing in a factory assembling things in a line.'

There was no other house in sight from the farm: it was truly isolated.

'You'll get used to that,' said Mr O'Brien. 'We never think a thing of it. And there's a bus to town two days a week.'

Kevin nodded. 'Two days a week!' He imagined Sadie's voice and her eyes round with horror at the restriction of only being able to go into the town on two days, and even then it was a small market town. He had Sadie's voice in his head most of the day, just as if she was standing at his elbow making comments.

'A grocery van calls on a Friday, I believe,' said Mr O'Brien. 'But my wife could tell you more about that. And then there's eggs and milk from the farm.'

'That's not so bad, eggs and milk,' said Sadie's voice, 'but what if I take a sudden notion for a bag of fish and chips?'

Mr O'Brien looked at Kevin's face beside him. 'You think you'd like the life, don't you? I mean, it wouldn't be any good coming if you didn't.'

'I think I'd like it all right,' said Kevin slowly. 'But it's a big step, you know. I have to think.'

'Of course. You can't decide these things in a flash. Your whole life's involved.'

His whole life. He had not thought of it like that but yes, it was true, once he came, it would be final, for he would not be able to put his family out of their home because he took a notion to change his job. And if Sadie did not come he would lose her for good. She had written to say that she did not want to, that she was afraid it would not work, and he thought she was right.

'Well, what did you think of it?' Brede demanded as soon as he opened the door. 'Isn't it a beautiful place?'

'Great,' he said.

'And Mr and Mrs O'Brien, sure aren't they the loveliest people?'

'They're very nice. I got on well with them.'

'Good,' said Mrs McCoy. She nodded with contentment.

'We're dying to see it on Saturday.'

'Saturday?' repeated Kevin.

'We're all going down to see it,' said Mrs McCoy. 'All of us. Robert has fixed it.'

'But I haven't said yes,' cried Kevin.

'You'll not be thinking of saying no now, will you?' said his mother, stricken at the thought that this haven of peace would be denied her.

Kevin looked out at the back yard and thought of the fields he had walked through that day and could not blame her. She deserved a change of fortune. But he was angry with Robert arranging for the family to go before Kevin had made up his mind. He had known Kevin was still swithering and was trying to push him. Kevin hated being pushed.

He told Robert so on Saturday when his family were running around the farm shouting and laughing and they were walking alone together.

'You shouldn't have done that, Robert. Let them see all this first.' He waved his hand. 'How could I disappoint them now?'

'I didn't think I was doing any harm, Kevin. After all, you wouldn't be wanting to deny them the chance of getting out of that hole in Belfast to live in the fresh air, would you?'

'It's not that easy, Robert, and you know it.' Kevin forced himself to keep calm. 'I have Sadie to think of.'

'But there's your mother and Brede and seven children to think of too.'

'Sadie's my wife.'

'But she's only one against nine.'

'I don't see it as a game of numbers. I'm torn right up the middle between the two.'

They walked a little way in silence, then Robert said, 'I'd never let my mother down. When you think what they do for you.'

'You'd put her before Brede?'

'I'm sure Brede wouldn't see it that way. She'd want me to do the right thing by my mother.'

Brede might. Kevin hoped she would. He felt glum inside, hoped now that she would be happy, that Robert would not disappoint her. There would not be much excitement in their union, but perhaps neither wanted that. He had excitement with Sadie, a feeling of freshness, of wonder. He might never find the same thing again. He kicked a clump of grass.

Brede came running up from behind and slipped between them. She took a hand of each.

'I'm glad to see the two of you becoming friends,' she said. She smiled up at Robert. Kevin said nothing. He thought that he and Robert might easily clash, for Robert could not understand there were other ways of seeing things than his, other lives to be lived. He could not understand how Kevin had come to marry a Protestant girl in the first place and get himself into such a mess.

'Gerald loves the animals,' said Brede. 'He's talking to Mr O'Brien in the cow shed right now.'

'Gerald might love the animals,' said Kevin, 'but that's not going to turn him into a saint.' At once he was sorry he had spoken so sourly and brought back the sadness into Brede's eyes.

They found their mother drinking tea and eating sultana cake in the Burkes' kitchen.

'This is just great,' sighed Mrs McCoy. 'A whole new life waiting for us. The children are all mad on it. They've never seen the like. And I think it'll be the making of Gerald.'

'We'll have to wait and see about that,' said Kevin. 'Just because he likes a few cows!'

'Cup of tea, Kevin?' asked Mrs Burke.

'No thanks. I'll go on over and have a chat with Mr O'Brien.'

'Kevin?' his mother called anxiously. He looked back from the doorway. 'You'll not be turning it down?'

'So what do you say to it now, Kevin?' said Mr O'Brien, settling himself in his leather armchair and lighting his pipe. 'Your family seem keen.'

'They're dead keen.'

'And that young brother of yours is going to make a good cowman I'll bet. He tells me he's sixteen in the summer so I've promised him a job.'

'Would you take him instead of me?' said Kevin suddenly, and smothered the guilt he felt at offering Gerald to anyone, knowing what he knew about him.

Mr O'Brien lifted the match away from his pipe. 'Take him

instead of you? But I want you both. He's only a young lad.'

Kevin sighed. It would have been too much to hope that he could put Gerald into his place. Gerald, who could scarcely keep out of trouble for two days at a time and would only earn a few pounds to start with. Kevin put a hand to his head. A pulse beat at the back of his temple like a loud tattoo. He did not know any longer what to think.

'There's something the matter, lad, isn't there?' The match burnt Mr O'Brien's fingers. He tossed it into the hearth, laid his pipe aside. 'Why don't you tell me about it? I'm a reasonable man.'

'I don't know what you can do,' said Kevin, 'but I'll tell you.'

Chapter Twenty-three

Sadie sat slumped in the train on the way home, her eyes closed, her mind automatically ticking off the stops on the line, so that when hers came she got up, moved to the opening doors and stepped on to the platform. She moved like a robot. That was how she felt after a long Friday at the supermarket, trapped under the fluorescent lights with the noise and smell of people around her making her feel that she could scarcely breathe or think. She thought of Kevin's letter in which he had told her about Tyrone, the green fields, the horses cropping the grass, the red brick barns, the smell of hay. The station smelt foul and was littered with papers dropped by hurrying, indifferent people. She gave her ticket into the grubby hand of the ticket collector and walked down the street, her arms weighed down by the heavy bags of groceries.

Rita was sitting on a high stool in the kitchen smoking a cigarette and flicking ash into the sink. Dirty dishes straggled across the draining board, not even properly stacked, but just lying where they had been dumped. There were usually dishes there when she came in, but this evening Sadie felt irritated by the sight of them and of Rita sitting on the stool with her legs crossed and a cigarette in her mouth.

'You might have done the dishes,' she snapped, immediately hearing her mother's voice in hers. Her mother had said the same thing many a time when she had come home to find Sadie sitting in the kitchen not even noticing that there was a pile of dishes waiting to be washed. Sadie sighed, fed up with herself, and Rita, and the dirty kitchen.

'I meant to,' said Rita good-naturedly. 'I forgot. I'll do them in a sec. What've you got?' She looked down at Sadie's bag.

'A chicken. Half-price. Skin's a bit torn but it's O.K. apart from that.'

'Smashing. How're you going to do it?'

'Roast it, I suppose,' said Sadie sourly, but Rita did not notice the sourness in her voice. She continued to sit on the stool and smoke whilst Sadie unpacked the groceries from the bags. She did all the shopping for the flat now and most of the cooking too, preferring it that way since the other two burnt or messed up the simplest dish. Rita prattled on about the latest gossip from the shop but Sadie did not listen. Her mind ran on with its own thoughts.

This life was doing her no good. She was getting all bitter and sour inside, finding faults with the girls, but they were all right, in their own way. The trouble was their way wasn't for her. She didn't want to share a flat with a couple of girls at all. She wanted to live with Kevin.

Kevin looked away from his mother's trembling hands. She held them clasped in front of her to steady them.

'Glory be to God!' she spoke in barely more than a whisper. 'I never thought I'd see the day when my eldest son would desert me in my hour of need.'

'But ma,' he said patiently, 'I have a wife to think of.'

'But she's a Protestant.'

'She's still my wife.' He looked his mother full in the face again, not liking the light in her eyes, but not looking away this time. 'We were married in the church.'

'No good'll come of a union like that.'

'Why not?' he asked quietly. 'It's up to us to make the good.'

'You'd have been better off with a girl of your own faith.'

'Perhaps. But it was Sadie I wanted –'

'Bah! What was she? Nothing but a stupid little baggage that ran about the streets making trouble. I never thought you'd stoop to the likes of her –'

'Stop it!' Now he was shouting, and he had never shouted before at his mother. He calmed, went on, 'I'm sorry, I didn't mean to shout, but I couldn't listen to you talk like that about Sadie.'

His mother was crying now, rocking herself and moaning about her lot and the terrible troubles she had had to bear. He had never seen her like this, she had been so calm when he was a child, the rock everyone had leant on and expected never to change, a peaceful, moderate woman who made few demands on others. Now she was querulous and demanding, but he could not blame her. He went to her, put his hands on her shaking shoulders. She put a roughened hand over his, grasping it eagerly, and hopefully.

'You won't leave me, will you, son?'

'Ma –' He closed his eyes.

'I need you, Kevin. You're the only son I can depend on. You can't go!'

'I must.'

She took her hand away, he removed his from her shoulders.

'You can still go to Tyrone,' he said. 'Mr O'Brien is willing to let you all live there as long as Gerald works for him and Michael helps out at week-ends and holidays.'

'Gerald! What use is he? He'll be in jail before he's much older.'

'Ach, don't talk that way about him, ma. Give him a chance. Maybe the farm'll straighten him out rightly.'

'He's past straightening out.' Her eyes were dry now, her voice steadier, and she was facing this fact of life as she had done many in the past, without flinching, not trying to escape the reality of it. 'Sure I know my own son. He was a devil from the day he was born but with all the fighting and blood that's been spilt he's been turned into something worse.'

Kevin was silent, recognising the truth of his mother's words.

'I'm leaving, Rita,' said Sadie. She laid the last package on the table.

'Leaving?'

'Tomorrow.'

'But what for?' asked Rita, still astonished. 'Is it because of the dishes?' She jumped off the stool. 'I'll do them now. Look, Sadie, you don't need to go on account of that. I know you get fed up with us at times –'

'It's not because of that.' Sadie switched on the oven, took the chicken, pulled out the cellophane bag containing its innards and wiped down the skin. 'I'm leaving London.'

'Leaving London? But I thought you liked it. We have a great time, don't we? And there's Joe.'

'I don't want Joe.' Sadie wrapped the chicken in tin foil, folding and tucking in the ends carefully. 'I want Kevin.'

'Kevin!'

'You don't have to go repeating everything I say,' said Sadie irritably.

'But you're not going to go for that deal with his family and all that, are you?'

'Why not? Why shouldn't I?'

'But, Sadie, have you thought?' Rita lit another cigarette, climbed back up on to the stool.

'Of course I've thought.'

'You'd live with his mother and sister and all those kids?' Rita's eyes goggled with disbelief.

'There's worse ways to live,' said Sadie. 'Anyway, there's all that lovely country and fresh air.'

'I never thought you liked the country much.'

'Well, I do now,' said Sadie and put the chicken into the oven even though it was not yet hot. She faced Rita. 'I'm going to pack.'

'Brede will be with you,' said Kevin, feeling guilty at the thought of Brede always carrying the burden, of having to be the one who would be there in times of trouble. Brede would never escape. But he must! He must go back to Sadie or else he would lose her. 'She and Robert can keep an eye on Gerald.'

'They'll not stop Gerald doing what he wants.'

'And neither would I.'

'No, maybe not,' his mother admitted. 'But I'd have you by me and I wouldn't need to depend on Gerald. How can I think of him as the bread-winner? Anyway, what'll he earn at his age?'

'I'll send you something every week, ma.'

'What can you send me?'

'A couple of pounds. Three?'

'Even so . . .' Her voice was turning querulous again. It was her son she wanted, not his money, though she would need that too with all the children to feed and clothe.

'And Mr O'Brien said you could have a job working for Mrs O'Brien in the house, helping with the cooking and that.'

'*I* could have a job? Have I not enough to do with all those children? Dear God, but I never thought I'd see the day when you'd be as cruel to me! Don't you think I've done enough work in my life scrubbing and cooking and slaving for the lot of youse without having to go into another woman's house and do the same for her?'

'I know, ma, and I'm sorry.' He turned away from her. He felt helpless, he did not know what to say to her, he was letting her down, in her eyes at least, and she probably deserved something better after all the bad luck and hard work in her life. But there was still Sadie, his wife. And there was his own life. 'I'm sorry,' he repeated.

Sadie did not sleep on the crossing. She stretched out on a settee in the lounge for a while but the excitement in her stomach would not let her lie at peace. She put on her coat and patrolled the deck watching the dark glint of the water running beneath the ship. In a few hours she would be back in Belfast amongst the people she had grown up with and the sound of familiar voices round her. There would be the sound of gun-fire and bombs too but those she did not think of tonight as the boat carried her steadily closer to the Irish shore.

In the morning she was first down the gangway, running out through the shed and into the street, dodging porters and dockers and cars. She ran all the way home banging her suitcase against her leg as she ran. With her she had brought only clothes, leaving with Rita their dishes and linen.

Her mother was frying bacon and eggs in the kitchen, the same flowered wrap-around apron girdling her hips, the same pink turban wound about her rollered head.

'Sadie! For dear sake!' Mrs Jackson dropped the fish slice on the floor.

'Ma!' Sadie flung her arms round her mother's neck and hugged her.

Mr Jackson, brought downstairs by the noise, arrived in his vest and trousers, with his braces dangling.

'Is it you, Sadie?'

'Who else?' she cried. 'Have I changed that much?'

' 'Deed you don't look as if you've changed one bit,' said her mother, picking up the fish slice to flip over a bit of bacon in the pan. 'You're hair's all over the place and you've the same pair of jeans on you. You didn't tell us when you were leaving and you didn't tell us when you were coming back.'

'Are you pleased to see me though?' asked Sadie.

'Aye well, I suppose I am right enough.'

Sadie grinned. She would never get a fuller admission than that from her mother. In a moment she would be sniffing and sighing and telling Sadie she was a sore trial, but right now she was half smiling and reaching for another rasher of bacon to toss into the pan for her returned daughter.

'We'll say no more now you're back,' said Mr Jackson.

'We'll let bygones be bygones. But you must know you caused us a sore bit of trouble.'

'I'm sorry,' said Sadie, edging round her mother to pinch a piece of bacon from the pan. 'I'm starved. Smell's gorgeous.'

'No, you don't change, do you?' said her mother, well enough pleased. 'We knew you'd see the light about that boy soon enough, but you had to find out for yourself. You can't tell kids anything.' Mrs Jackson sniffed, turned off the gas and began to dish out the breakfast.

Sadie sat at the table, quiet now. 'How'd you mean, I'd find out for myself?'

'That you'd made a mistake of course,' said her father.

'What else?'

'But I don't think I did make one,' said Sadie.

'What?' Mrs Jackson laid her hand against her thin neck between the edges of the apron. 'Do you mean –?'

'I'm still married,' said Sadie, starting to eat. The bacon was delicious, lean and crisp, just as she liked it, and the fried potato bread melted in her mouth. 'This potato bread tastes good. Boys, I really missed it in London.'

Her mother and father were not eating: they were watching her with wonder and apprehension.

'Do you mean to say you're still living with that Mick and you've got the nerve to come back here?' said her father.

'Aye well, I'm on my way down to Tyrone. We're going to be living on a farm there.'

Mr and Mrs Jackson looked at one another warily. Yes, Sadie was a sore trial, and only last night Tommy had told them he was leaving next month for Australia.

'Tyrone,' said Mrs Jackson, as if it were the moon. 'What're you going there for?'

'Kevin's mother comes from there. We're going to be living next door to her, and his sister, and brother-in-law, and seven or eight other brothers and sisters,' Sadie added, unable to resist watching their reaction.

'With all them Micks?' Mr Jackson's horror made him pale. 'You're stupider than I ever thought you were, Sadie Jackson. I used to think you were smart!' He shook his head.

Sadie finished her breakfast, took a slice of bread from the packet on the table, and spread it with butter. She needed food inside her before she faced the journey to Tyrone, though it was not the journey that bothered her, it was the arrival.

'And did you think you'd be welcome here when you were on your way to take up with a bunch of Micks?' Her mother put her hands over her face. 'It's too much! I don't know what we did to deserve it.'

'Probably nothing, ma.' Sadie touched her arm. 'Come on now, don't take on so. I'll be all right.'

'But what about us?'

'Your ma's right, Sadie,' said Mr Jackson, 'it's us that suffers. Everybody was talking about you round here when you went off with him.'

'You'd think they'd enough to talk about.' Sadie got up. 'What with people getting killed and all that. You'd think they wouldn't care about two people wanting to marry one another.'

'Depends what people,' said Mr Jackson.

'You needn't worry, I'll be leaving soon. Tommy gone to work?'

'Yes. And he's going to Australia next month and all.'

'I'd like to see him,' said Sadie. 'I'll leave my address for him.'

Her mother and father sat at the table drinking their tea, letting their food grow cold and congealed on the plates. They looked miserable. Sadie opened her mouth, then closed it again not knowing what she could say to them. She sighed. Her mother scratched her head between the rollers and sniffed.

'I don't know,' said her father. 'I just don't know.'

Sadie put on her coat, lifted her suitcase. 'Nice seeing you again. I'll keep in touch.'

The sun was shining, the birds twittering in the branches overhead. They were gradually returning after the long winter, and the branches were thickening with buds.

'Spring,' said Brede happily. 'It's coming.'

'Yes, it feels like it,' said Kevin, tipping his head back to look at the white and blue sky. 'And then you'll have the summer and you'll get fat and brown and when I come back I won't know you.'

'Don't you wish you weren't going away?'

'I suppose so, a bit. But I'm going to see Sadie, Brede. That makes the difference.'

Brede nodded. She was married now to Robert, snug in her little cottage, and whenever she looked out at the grass and trees and heard the peaceful sound of the countryside she could scarcely believe it. Kevin had come with them to help them settle in but tomorrow he would go and she would miss him.

'You'll do your best by ma?' said Kevin with a sigh. 'But of course you will. I don't have to ask.'

'She'll get over it, Kevin.'

'Ah well, she may not, but what can I do?'

Mrs McCoy had started at the farmhouse. She returned each afternoon to look reproachfully at Kevin complaining that her back was aching and doubting if she'd last to see the spring come into full flower. But on the whole she was happier, relieved at last to have left the town and its cruel streets behind. 'I never should have left Tyrone at all,' she said. 'I'd have done better to have married a local boy and stayed where I belonged.'

Brede glanced over by the road. 'Kevin,' she cried out, pointing, making him turn his head, 'Look! Someone's coming. It looks like –'

'Sadie,' he said softly. Yes, it was her, walking with her head up, her fair hair fluttering around her face, a suitcase in her hand. He started to run towards her.

She dropped the suitcase and ran into his arms. He lifted her right off the ground, clasping her tightly against his chest.

'Sadie, oh Sadie!' He set her down, still holding on to her, to look into her face. 'It is you right enough. It's like a miracle.'

'Oh Kevin, it seems like ten years since I've seen you.' Sadie was half laughing, half crying.

'I was coming to you tomorrow,' he said. 'I just came to settle in the family.'

'But I've come to live with you.'

'You have?'

'You did ask me?'

'Yes. But since then –'

'Kevin,' his mother called again.

They turned. Mrs McCoy stood beside Brede on the path.

'Kevin,' his mother called again.

'Come on, Sadie.' Kevin took Sadie's hand. 'You must meet my mother.'

As they approached Brede and her mother, Brede said, 'Hello, Sadie, nice to see you.' Mrs McCoy stared hard at Sadie, unblinking and unsmiling.

'Ma, this is Sadie,' said Kevin.

'Hello, Mrs McCoy,' said Sadie.

Mrs McCoy said nothing. She stood like a statue, frozen.

'Have you come to stay with us, Sadie?' asked Brede. 'I hope you have. We'd like it very much indeed.'

'She's not staying,' said Kevin. 'We're leaving this afternoon. Together.' Sadie glanced up at him quickly; he squeezed her hand.

'Oh!' Brede was disappointed. 'Where are you going?'

'We don't know yet,' he said. 'Would you like to make Sadie a cup of tea, Brede?'

'Surely.' Brede went off to her cottage.

Mrs McCoy pulled her coat more tightly around her. 'I'm away back to my work, Kevin,' she said. 'You'll come and say good-bye before you go?'

He nodded. She gave Sadie a last look, then walked off along the track towards the farmhouse.

'I don't think I hit it off with your mother,' said Sadie ruefully.

'You'd no chance to, and you never would. We could never live here, love. We'd have no chance at all. I'd be a fool if I ever thought we had.'

'I was willing to try.'

'I know. And I'm grateful to you for that.'

He put his arms around her and she leant against him, sheltering from the wind. She looked at the countryside spread out before them. 'It's a pity in a way,' she said. 'It's so peaceful here after London. Like you said in your letter.'

'Yes, it's peaceful,' he said. 'But that's not everything. And there are other peaceful places, Sadie. We'll find one. Of our own.'

Also by Joan Lingard

TUG OF WAR

Forced to flee Latvia with their family, twins Astra and Hugo journey to Germany in carts, on foot and subsequently by boat, where they are attacked by planes from above and submarines from below. At a crowded station, Hugo is injured and separated from his family and thereafter fate takes brother and sister in different directions. In their constant search for each other, Hugo fears that his family might be dead; Astra fears that Hugo might be trapped behind the Iron Curtain, but neither gives up hope.

Read more in Puffin

For complete information about books available from Puffin – and Penguin – and how to order them, contact us at the appropriate address below. Please note that for copyright reasons the selection of books varies from country to country.

www.puffin.co.uk

In the United Kingdom: Please write to Dept EP, Penguin Books Ltd, Bath Road, Harmondsworth, West Drayton, Middlesex UB7 ODA

In the United States: Please write to Penguin Putnam Inc., P.O. Box 12289, Dept B, Newark, New Jersey 07101–5289 or call 1–800–788–6262

In Canada: Please write to Penguin Books Canada Ltd, 10 Alcorn Avenue, Suite 300, Toronto, Ontario M4V 3B2

In Australia: Please write to Penguin Books Australia Ltd, P.O. Box 257, Ringwood, Victoria 3134

In New Zealand: Please write to Penguin Books (NZ) Ltd, Private Bag 102902, North Shore Mail Centre, Auckland 10

In India: Please write to Penguin Books India Pvt Ltd, 11 Panscheel Shopping Centre, Panscheel Park, New Delhi 110 017

In the Netherlands: Please write to Penguin Books Netherlands bv, Postbus 3507, NL–1001 AH Amsterdam

In Germany: Please write to Penguin Books Deutschland GmbH, Metzlerstrasse 26, 60594 Frankfurt am Main

In Spain: Please write to Penguin Books S. A., Bravo Murillo 19, 1° B, 28015 Madrid

In Italy: Please write to Penguin Italia s.r.l., Via Felice Casati 20, I–20124 Milano

In France: Please write to Penguin France S. A., 17 rue Lejeune, F–31000 Toulouse

In Japan: Please write to Penguin Books Japan, Ishikiribashi Building, 2–5–4, Suido, Bunkyo-ku, Tokyo 112

In South Africa: Please write to Longman Penguin Southern Africa (Pty) Ltd, Private Bag X08, Bertsham 2013